Rebekah

Doug Sparks

Rebekah Publishing
Box 713 • Gunnison, Colorado 81230

Rebekah Publishing
Box 713
Gunnison, Colorado 81230
Phone: 1-877-790-4588
www.Rebekahbooks.com

Edited by Ann Marie Gordon
Cover and interior design by Jan Melvin

ISBN 0-9720471-0-7
Library of Congress Control Number 2002091418

1   2   3   4   02   03   04   05

Dedicated to the special women in my life:

Candace, my wife. A true partner, friend, and excellent leader.
My mother, Eloise Sparks. A mission fulfilled.
My mother-in-law, Til Cortesi. A faithful woman of prayer.
My daughters, Stephanie and Elisabeth. A wonderful road lies ahead.
Mariel "Mama" Hijink. My pastor, teacher, counselor, friend, and mentor.

Acknowledgments

This is a work of fiction. The names, events, and characters are purely a product of the author's imagination. However, the underlying issues of the role of women in the church, biased scriptural interpretation, and faulty translation are not fiction; they are very real.

David Hamilton, a very fine Bible scholar, spent nearly a decade researching minute details of early manuscripts, cross-referencing thousands of topics and wading fearlessly into uncharted waters of Greek, Roman, and Jewish history, searching for the non-biased truth about the role women had in the primitive church. His work is summarized in the book Why Not Women? See the suggested reading list at the end of the book for more resource information.

As in any first-time effort, the author was plagued with a plethora of fears and doubts. Jane, Becca, Deyon, and Cheri gave needed encouragement to press on. Thanks.

Ann Marie Gordon took her red pen to an amorphous mass of words and helped create a story. The unlit journey is not so daunting when someone with you knows the way.

Jane Overstreet, my boss at Development Associates International, first suggested the idea of writing something on the women in leadership. Jane had created a character named Rebekah for some teaching she did in India. With Jane's encouragement I took her idea and built a story.

Chapter One
Cairo, Egypt 2000

Rebekah strode briskly up the front steps of the church taking the steps two at a time. Her long, bushy hair clasped back bounced easily on her shoulders. It was difficult to get away from her medical clinic at any set time. There were always last minute emergencies; today was no exception. The bus was running behind schedule and now she was twenty minutes late.

She reached the heavy mahogany door and pushed down on the handle. As usual, the door didn't budge. She pressed down on the handle harder and bumped the door with her slender hip. It opened slightly. Using her shoulder and all one hundred and fifteen pounds of weight to shove the huge door, she opened it just enough to slip past. The air in the darkened foyer was a pleasant contrast to the furnace-like heat outside. She paused in the coolness to catch her breath and let her eyes adjust to the dimly lit hallway which ran parallel to the main sanctuary and led to Pastor Mounir Habib's private office.

The door to Pastor Habib's outer office was wide open; she heard voices coming from the adjoining room. She quickly stepped through the empty office and without hesitation entered the conference room.

All discussion stopped as she came through the door. Every head turned to look at her. Rebekah smiled at Reverend Habib. He was bent over chatting with one of the men, his hands resting on the highly polished table.

"I am sorry for being late, it was difficult getting away from my clinic on short notice," she said to Pastor Habib.

Reverend Habib stood up and motioned for her to come in; he pulled out a chair at the head of the table. Moving toward the empty seat Rebekah glanced around the room. She recognized the eight men sitting at the table; they were the local church elders. No one looked at her directly; a few stole a quick glance and returned their gaze downward. The men reminded her of sunflowers drooping on the end of stalks after the sun had passed them by, heads sagging in unison. Only Dr. Thomas Asbury sitting in the back, his arms folded across his chest, had his gaze fixed on Rebekah.

Reverend Habib looked at Dr. Asbury, spread his arms wide open and nodded toward the back of the room, then sat down. Thomas rose from his seat and walked slowly toward Rebekah. "Thank you, Rebekah, for coming on such short notice. I am Dr. Thomas Asbury, the new Executive Director for our denomination. We have not been introduced formally." His voice was silky smooth. He adjusted his necktie and buttoned his suit jacket as he slowly made his way to where she sat.

Thomas made a mental note of what Rebekah was wearing. He believed ones dress was a dead giveaway to their inner workings. She wore a simple white blouse, buttoned up higher than it should have been. Loose black dress slacks and matching open-toed sandals. The clothes were nice, not expensive but not cheap.

He noticed her toes were perfectly aligned, none sticking out of sequence. Nails painted an opaque off-white, no chips. He looked directly into her ebony eyes. They were clear and bright like two pieces of polished coal. Her hair was equally black and unusually thick and curly. It was pulled back, bundled together with a heavy silver clasp at the nap of her neck.

Her skin was a very light brown, the color you would get if you mixed a tiny bit of molasses with heavy cream. There was also a tinge of the Mediterranean olive-green. No blemishes, no wrinkles, just pure supple skin. Rebekah was without any makeup or jewelry, with the exception of a tiny silver necklace around her smooth neck.

Thomas slowed his pace, he needed time to evaluate his impressions. She certainly had an inborn elegance that no school could teach. And she had a presence or was it an attitude? Since her entrance every man in the room seemed to take a comfortable backseat to her. Dr. Asbury was used to seeing this among the rich, the powerful, and the famous, but not from a young woman with none of these qualities of greatness. Thomas was now wary.

Rebekah looked up; Dr. Asbury stopped next to her chair. She smelled his cologne, saw his beautifully tailored navy blue suit, the shiny black shoes, and belt. His belt had an oversized gold buckle. Dr. Asbury's blonde hair and boyish face put her at ease for a moment. She then looked directly into his emotionless, pale blue eyes. For no obvious reason a chill crept down her spine. Her coal black eyes darted around the room trying to find a friendly face to bolster her. There was none. Rebekah felt panic rise within — the feeling a rodent has knowing it's in the deadly sights of a predator with no hope of escape.

"As you know, I have been in Egypt a fairly short time. It is my desire — no, my solemn obligation to make sure that each and every church in this denomination is complying fully with Scripture. I came to one of your meetings some time ago and was deeply disturbed to observe you teaching publicly and exercising leadership over men." His voice was starting to get higher and louder.

"The Apostle Paul makes it absolutely clear that women are to be silent in the church. They are most certainly not to have any authority over men nor to have any public ministry. You have purposely usurped power and authority from the rightful leaders. Such an example will lead the faithful away from obvious Biblical truth." Small bits of spittle were launched from his angry lips with each word.

"You have used your beauty, charm, and pleasant speech to deceive. Others may have been bewitched by you, but not me." He looked coldly at the men at the table. "Such acts of defiance and rebellion will not be tolerated in this church. Is that understood?" he hissed.

Dr. Asbury turned his livid face toward Pastor Habib and then at each man sitting at the table. "You men are a disgrace to your Lord and this church by allowing this to happen. Have you no backbone to stand up to this woman? Have you no sense of righteousness, no fundamental commitment to truth? Who has deceived you?" Thomas shouted at the men. Their heads drooped lower in unison, trying to duck the verbal blows.

Dr. Asbury returned his violent gaze to Rebekah. "You will never speak in this church again, you will never lead or have any public ministry — ever. Do you understand?" He turned and glared at Mounir Habib. "Is that clear Pastor Habib?"

"Yes, sir," Mounir whispered to his folded hands.

Rebekah sat in front of the elders feeling humiliated, betrayed, and stunned. Surely they were not serious. She had been friends with each of the elders for several years. They knew her. Some had even attended her teaching sessions and complimented her on what a gifted teacher she was. She always sought permission before starting a new class or group.

When Dr. Asbury finished his tirade Rebekah, and every other woman in the congregation, had been stripped of any meaningful roles, any public involvement, any dignity, or value in the church. Thomas Asbury felt good about what he had just done. He had set an example for the elders; he had kept God's word pure and undefiled.

Rebekah sat in a dazed stupor. She felt as if someone had punched her in the stomach; she could hardly breathe. Without saying a word Rebekah stood; with her head lowered, legs weak, and tears dripping from her chin she stumbled out the office door and fled down the dark hallway.

Over the next days and weeks she was emotionally numb. Her work as a doctor demanded her full attention, so she went through the paces, keeping her mind and body busy.

Chapter Two

It had been six months since the elders' meeting, Rebekah tried hard to forget the past and move forward with her life. A thin veil of civility lightly covered her raw hurt and anger. The one common thread throughout her life — the thread that brought the agony, loneliness, guilt, rejection, betrayal, and suffering — was somehow all tied to being a woman; she hated herself for being one; sometimes she hated God for making her one. The ember of self-hatred smoldered under a blanket of shame.

She was emotionally and physically exhausted. In Egypt a doctor is paid only about one hundred dollars per month from the government to work at the hospitals. To make enough money to live, doctors had to open private clinics to service paying clients. Her work was very demanding — a full schedule at the government hospital during the days and her private clinic in the evenings — a hectic lifestyle that left her feeling as dry as the desert sand.

To rejuvenate her spirit, Rebekah took a day off and headed for a special place she knew on the river. The chance to get out of Cairo did not happen often, but on this day she needed to get away.

Outside the city the congested road split: the left fork led to the Sinai desert; the road to the right followed the Nile River. After many stops and several miles, the bus slowed and pulled to a halt. A cloud of dust enveloped Rebekah as she stepped off the decrepit vehicle and walked quickly to the other side of the small dirt road. The driver gave her a toothless smile and a friendly salute as he coaxed the bus forward.

The sunshine on her shoulders felt good. She stood for a moment pausing to look down on the mighty Nile. The moving water was peaceful and majestic.

She walked a few hundred yards past the end of the trail and found the flat rocks, each one jutting further out into the river. A short jump from one stone to the next brought Rebekah well away from the shore.

She removed her sandals and gently lowered her feet into the water. It surprised her how cold the water felt at first and how quickly she grew accustomed to it.

This was exactly what she needed. Though able to effortlessly remove the daypack from her shoulders, the heaviness of her heart was not as easily discarded.

All she wanted was peace and quiet. As the din of busyness settled from her mind, she heard voices. She sat up and cupped her hands to the side of her face and looked hard. A small group of children played in the water on the far bank more than a quarter of a mile away. She saw the water splashing as they ran after one another, squealing in delight. The actual words the children shouted to one another were not discernable: but Rebekah knew the language of children having fun.

Leaning back on the blanket, she closed her eyes. Her mind easily went back to her days of youthful freedom and carefree play. She grew up on the banks of the Nile four hundred miles upstream. The water there ran cooler and cleaner. As a young girl, she often played in the river with her older brothers on hot summer days. Just as these children were doing, nearly naked, she splashed and ran as hard as she could to catch her brothers and their friends. It was such innocence and joy.

Recalling the days of her youth, Rebekah tried to conjure up what her mother's face looked like, her father's, her brothers'. More than fifteen years had passed since she had seen them. Then like the hot desert wind that blew without warning, she was flooded with fear. She sensed danger.

Rebekah sat up quickly and spun around. She looked carefully all along the brush-covered hillside directly in back of her, but she could see no one. The fright set her heart racing wildly. She told herself to relax; no one was going to hurt her again; there was no danger. But rarely did she relax; there was an inner turmoil that bubbled to the surface whenever she tried to be quiet. She took a long drink from her water bottle, straightened out the blanket, and once again found comfort in the warm sun and cool water.

Soon her exhaustion overcame her fears and Rebekah fell asleep on the rock. At first it was a peaceful sleep, but soon the same torturous dream seeped up from the subconscious as it had so often.

In her recurring nightmare, she was in a dark room lying on a comfortable bed. She was not quite asleep but not fully awake. There was a presence with her and although she could not see it, she could sense it coming toward her. A black, formless mass gradually enveloped her. Starting at her feet, it ascended over her slowly, inching its way up her body. As it engulfed her more and more, she felt its weight pressing on her, gently at first, like a cloud settling upon a mountain peak.

The black cloud slowly began pressing the life from her. In a frightening panic she opened her mouth to cry for help but could not draw in any air; her mouth hung open in a silent scream. Her bulging eyes were wild with fright; her useless arms and legs were pinned to the mattress. Terror pumped through her veins; she knew the black monster meant to destroy her.

Rebekah awoke with a great shutter and twitch of her body fighting the invisible enemy. Still lying on the blanket, beads of perspiration dotted her furrowed forehead. She gasped for air. A quiet groan came from deep within her as she sat up slowly. Splashing river water on her face, she took several deep breaths and rested her head on her knees. "When will this ever end?" she thought to herself.

Perhaps it was seeing the children playing at the water's edge that prompted the painful memories of her youth. When she was thirteen, one of her older brother's friends, Abdel, began coming to her house. He should have been working in the fields with the men of her village and the other boys his age. He would somehow managed to slip away and come to her home. Rebekah figured out much later that he must have watched her house and waited for her mother to leave, because he knew when she was alone.

At first she thought he was just being friendly. After several harmless visits Rebekah was not paying much attention when she saw him come up to the house. He came up behind her and put his strong arms around her waist and began kissing her neck. Rebekah froze; she had never been touched this way by a man. He grabbed her forcefully; one arm around her neck the other tightly around her waist he began to pull her backwards.

Rebekah twisted and squirmed her body with all her strength, she reached for his farmer hands to push them away, but they were like vice-grips. She opened her mouth wide to scream for help but before any sound came out a rough, calloused hand clamped it tight. Careful not to let any fingers get in harms way.

Without much effort, Abdel, who outweighed her by more than one hundred twenty pounds, drug her toward the rear of the house. At one point he paused to look out the window to make sure no one was coming. He relaxed his grip; she escaped for two running steps. Then her head snapped back like she had been hit with a baseball bat. Abdel had caught her by the hair and yanked with such force that one sandal flew off her foot and landed in the next room. He wrapped his hand firmly in her hair and began to drag. Rebekah whimpered and pleaded with him not to hurt her.

He responded with a sound that was part grunt and part laugh and continued dragging her into a dark back room where no one would hear her pitiful cries.

Abdel threw Rebekah on an old, dirty mattress that her older brother slept on. He pinned her head down by her hair and began to rip off her flimsy cotton dress with his free hand. Once she was naked he slowed his pace. He sat there looking at her pure, innocent body. She shut her eyes tight and blushed with shame. She could hear his breathing become heavy.

Abdel knelt on top of her and jammed both of his knees between her legs. He had already pulled up his galabeya, a loose-fitting robe worn by Egyptian men, and put his entire weight on her body. He purposefully rammed his shoulder up under her chin so she could not scream and pressed down on her throat with the same shoulder to cut off most of her air. Rebekah slowly lost consciousness and stopped struggling.

Rebekah lost track of time; she didn't know if the attack took two minutes or ten, all she knew was that her life would forever change. Abdel was suddenly quiet. He continued to lay on Rebekah, his stinking breath filling her nostrils and his wet saliva running down her neck. He raised himself up on one elbow and looked long and full at Rebekah, his lustful eyes still burning with passion, his lips twisted into a diabolical smile showing his crooked, yellow teeth.

Slowly he leaned close to Rebekah's ear and whispered, "If you ever tell anyone, I will come back and kill you." Rebekah didn't move or speak. Abdel pushed himself roughly off of her and stood by the mattress smiling at his naked prey, knowing he would be back for more. He took one final look and then strutted out the back door his head held high in victory.

Rebekah started to get up to make sure he was gone, but when she moved an intense pain shot through her groin. She looked down and saw blood smeared on the inside of her pale thighs. Bending forward she saw a small circle of blood on the mattress where she now sat. She found her torn dress on the floor and put it on. She stood up slowly and limped to the bathroom.

She ran a sink full of water and began to frantically wash her face and neck with her trembling hands, she could still smell his rutting odor and sickening breath. Lifting her dress she saw the trail of blood now weaving its way down the inside of her legs. She grabbed a towel and began carefully wiping the crimson, innocent blood away. She suddenly felt dirty, the kind of dirt that no amount of water can ever cleanse.

Even now after all these years, Rebekah still had difficulty believing it actually happened. It was less painful to recall the repeated rapes, if she pretended to be an observer not the victim.

Rebekah was so ashamed, confused, and fearful that she told no one. He came back three times over the next two months. Every time he came for her she tried to escape, each time he found a way to corner her. Rebekah remembered the evil smirk on Abdel's face as he pinned her arms behind her and put his face close to hers, his brutish cracked lips kissing her neck, his dull eyes alive with excitement.

Finally, her mother came in from the fields unexpectedly one day just as the boy was leaving and questioned him forcefully. He stopped coming. Rebekah's mother looked at her suspiciously, but said nothing.

Rebekah remembered something frightening was happening within her body. She had no idea what the change was, but something was not normal. The continued sick feeling in her stomach and the vomiting each morning were uncommon for her. She had always been very healthy. One morning when she was in bed ill, her mother came and sat on the edge of the small straw mattress on the floor. "Rebekah, my precious child, what is the matter? You have not been yourself for many months now. You must tell me what has happened." Her voice was warm and soothing, full of love and motherly concern.

Lying with her back to her mother, she began to weep. She rolled over, burying her face in her mother's lap. Through the tears and sobs, she recounted the terror and pain of the repeated sexual assaults. Her mother sat quietly for a long time, thinking, holding her only daughter in her arms, tears running down her face.

Trying hard to control the emotion in her voice, her mother told her that if her father found out, he would have to kill her. In their village, the custom was to kill the daughter if she became pregnant without being married, regardless of the circumstances. Having an unwed, pregnant daughter brought shame to the family. She explained that to regain the family honor, the daughter must die at the hands of a male family member.

Rebekah protested that it was not her fault. Abdel was so much bigger and stronger and forced himself on her. "In our culture it does not matter whose fault it is," her mother said coldly. "The woman always carries the blame." Her mother told her not to tell anyone and left the room. Rebekah went weak with fear and burned with anger.

Weeks later, Rebekah recollected, her mother woke her early in the morning. She put her finger to her lips telling Rebekah to be quiet. They walked together through the empty, dirt streets of the village to the bus stop. They stood side-by-side, silent, fearful. When the bus arrived, Rebekah's mother went up the three steps to where the driver sat; she spoke to him in whispers and nodded toward Rebekah. The driver, somber, said nothing but looked down at Rebekah. Her mother returned down the steps gave her a small, pink plastic suitcase she had bought from a neighbor and placed a ticket in her hand. She kissed Rebekah on both cheeks, held her tight, then pushed her roughly toward the open bus door. Her mother did not look back and walked quickly around the corner out of sight.

Rebekah often wondered what story her mother told her father and brothers. What did she say to the neighbors? How did she explain her disappearance? She never knew the answers to these questions, but one thing is certain, her mother had paid an awful price to save her.

Rebekah's mouth went dry just recalling the heart-breaking departure from her mother and family. She reached over and took a long drink from her water bottle. Her heart was still beating rapidly. She tried consciously to think of something else, but like a compass needle always pointing north, her mind returned to the memories of the long bus ride. She remembered clutching the pink plastic suitcase to her side and tried to burn into her memory the face of her mother. The driver glanced at her in the overhead mirror every few minutes. The bus finally stopped in the center of Asyut, a large, dusty city overlooking the Nile. The driver motioned for her to follow him. He walked half a block toward the entrance to the bus station and stopped.

A woman came up behind them and said something to the driver, he glanced at Rebekah and left. "I am your mother's cousin," she said sternly, a look of disgust on her pinched lifeless face. Without saying another word, she turned and walked down the street. Rebekah had to hurry to catch up and had a hard time keeping up with the angry woman. It was clear to Rebekah, there would be little compassion or human warmth from her newfound relative. "You can stay here till the baby is born and not a day longer," were her first words once inside her dirty, smelly apartment.

Rebekah thought of the long, gloomy weeks and months of waiting, doing menial household chores, and getting bigger. Feeling something moving inside her was scary at first, but soon she became familiar with the routine within. Rebekah never had considered how she would feel toward the baby. She hated the boy who had done this to her ... the shame, the injustice, the blame, making her leave her family and friends and school. The hatred was raw and deep, but her feelings toward the child were different; she loved the life within.

Rebekah's memory of the birth was very foggy; thinking back on it brought no distinct impressions. It was a mass of mixed, mingled feelings of pain, of panic, not knowing what to expect, blood, screams, strangers shouting instructions. The scene was like an impressionistic painting, each dab of paint, one awful experience. She did remember the moment when the baby came, one of the attending women whispered to the others, "It's a boy."

The stern-faced woman shouting the orders immediately took the baby and wrapped him in a piece of an old sheet. It was a faded, threadbare rag with gray and yellow flowers barely visible. A piece of it had been left in the room. Rebekah took it and kept it in the pink plastic suitcase for several years. It was all she had left to remember her baby. The woman holding the newborn looked for a second at Rebekah and then rushed out of the room. Rebekah did not realize what was happening.

It slowly dawned on Rebekah that the child and woman were not going to return. Filled with panic and terror, she tried crawling after her baby, but several rough hands pushed her back on the bed and held her tight. She opened her mouth to scream for her child, but the sound that came out was so unhuman, so full of anguish, the women stopped and looked at each other and left the room with their heads bowed in shame.

Rebekah recalled lying in the small, dark bedroom wanting to die. Her young mother's heart broken, she turned her face to the wall and sobbed in body-heaving agony.

Rebekah shuddered as she remembered the heartache of her youth. Her past was an ever-present reminder of the torment of being a woman. She could not escape her lot in life, nor did she think she was dealing with it particularly well. She felt confused and overwhelmed.

Rebekah spent the entire day on the rock, reading and napping and reflecting. When the sun began to descend in the western sky, she looked at her watch and began folding the blanket, placing the books in her pack. Jumping from rock to rock, she made her way back to shore and slowly climbed the riverbank to catch the last bus home.

Overall, it had been a good day. She waited only a few minutes at the dirt bus stop, watching as the dilapidated vehicle slowly wound its way to where she stood. The door was already open; she stepped up, smiled at the driver, and found the only empty seat near the back. The bus lurched into gear and retraced the morning route, carrying its human cargo and the burdens they each concealed. The sun settled quietly on the western horizon; no one noticed.

A few days after the time spent at the river, Rebekah sat in her apartment twirling her long dark hair nervously between her fingers; she needed answers. Rebekah was certain the Lord had called her to use her talents and abilities and she wanted to obey. But how?

The worn Bible lay untouched on the stand by her bed. Before the encounter with Dr. Asbury she read it regularly; since the verbal mauling, it went unused. There was no desire to read a book that condemned her to a life of subservience and stripped her of value. The implications of such thinking wrapped themselves like tentacles around her soul. She felt her spirit being squeezed to death. How could a god of love and compassion be so cruel to women? Why was she forever paying a debt she didn't owe?

Chapter Three
Tulsa, Oklahoma 1984

The Piedmont Auditorium in downtown Tulsa is the only jewel in an otherwise desolate crown. What Tulsa lacks in genuine sophistication it tried buying with oil money. The Piedmont stands as a gaudy shrine in an attempt to appease the gods of culture. On this Friday night, two hours before the show was to begin, people were already flowing in wanting to get a good seat.

Gertrude and Margaret arrived by bus. They walked the short distance to the ground-level entrance. A doorman opened the glass doors and they cautiously made their way into unfamiliar territory. With the help of an usher, they found very good seats near the front. The show did not start for nearly two hours, but they wanted to get close to the stage so they could get a good look at T. Tucker Tiltun.

Margaret had a few crumbs of bread on her lower lip from a forbidden sandwich she had smuggled in and consumed bite-by-illegal-bite while Gertrude stood watch. Margaret felt a little naughty and a little proud that she had managed to elude the theater's food police.

Fifteen minutes before the program began, the auditorium was nearly full. Only a few seats in the center of the front rows remained roped off and empty. At precisely seven fifty-five, there was a stir as several ushers walked briskly down the aisle making way for a very handsome-looking family: the Asburys.

One of the ushers, a fat man in his sixties whose black uniform and white shirt made him look like a penguin breathing heavily from the forced march down the aisle, opened the roped-off section, stepped back, and, bowing slightly from his oversized waist, made a sweeping motion with his pudgy hand. The family of three filed in and sat down. The usher marched back up the aisle looking very pleased, very important.

"You know, Gertrude, it is wholesome Christian families like that," she nodded at the Asburys, "that make America great."

Gertrude could not immediately answer. She had just slipped a large piece of contraband banana into her mouth, but she shook her head vigorously in agreement, eyes wide with excitement.

The two overweight friends settled back to enjoy the evening.

Thomas Robert Asbury II sat quietly between his parents. Tommy Bob, as he was called, still wore the khaki pants, blue blazer, white shirt, and tie he had worn to school that day. At the Fraiser Academy, a private, elite school, he was required to wear "gentlemen's attire" each and every day. At sixteen years old, Tommy Bob was a very tall and handsome young man. He inherited the best genetic characteristics from each parent. Most people noticed his wonderfully pale blue eyes first, bright but troubled.

Tommy Bob did not have many close friends. He felt more comfortable withdrawing into his own private world. Often moody and irritable, people tended to stay away. When you are guarding secrets, you do not want people to get too close. So on the one hand his aloofness gave him what he wanted: space. But on the other hand it only added to his sense of isolation and loneliness.

No one but his parents knew he had been seeing a psychiatrist because of the depression and suicidal thoughts that plagued him. The cause of his depression proved elusive. Outwardly he seemed to have everything: a beautiful house, the best clothes, enrolled in one of the finest prep schools in the country, a swimming pool in his backyard ... anything imaginable that he wanted, he got.

The doctor suggested a trial of a new drug to control the adolescent depression and added regular therapy sessions to help Tommy Bob find out the cause of the depression. Thomas Sr. said okay to the drugs, but did not want his son seeing a "shrink." If people found out, it would soil his image as a tough, independent, successful oilman. His mother, Shirley, thought the drugs were a good idea. She had several small, full boxes and was really quite good at controlling her life with the use of drugs. Why just tonight she was sailing through an otherwise agonizing evening with her cheating husband, all due to the marriage-saving power of drugs.

It was during this time of meeting with the psychiatrist that Tommy Bob made his own discovery. He wasn't sure if it had anything to do with his depression or his anxieties, but he suspected it did. He was a homosexual.

He did not even know what it meant until he learned about it in health class at school. In a lecture on sexuality, the teacher explained that in certain situations, for unknown reasons, some people had a desire for those of the same sex rather than the opposite sex.

As soon as the teacher said the words, Tommy Bob began to perspire. He had to consciously breathe deeply and slowly to keep the fear of discovery under control. The teacher's words seemed to explode in his head; she was describing him. A couple of the boys in the class made rude comments and snickered. One boy raised his hand and asked, "What do they actually do to each other?" The teacher turned bright red with embarrassment and said, "We don't talk about such things in public." After class Tommy Bob sat alone in the library pondering this new revelation.

He had never had the typical male desires. Tommy did not like being around his father; he was so rough and harsh. Instead he enjoyed dressing up in his mother's clothing and creating fashion shows for her. It was all just innocent fun; besides, his mother encouraged him. She enjoyed the company. His father was not home very often.

When he was entering his early teenage years, the other boys talked about girls. Some actually claimed they had slept with one. No one really believed them, but it somehow made them more popular. Still, Tommy Bob had no desire for girls; it was the other older boys that he found himself thinking about.

Every time people talked about faggots, queers, or gays, Tommy Bob would tense up. He could not possibly let anyone know what was going on inside. He felt so guilty, so ashamed, so confused.

Sunday mornings made him feel the worst. In church, the preacher would shout angrily when talking about how the homosexuals were threatening to destroy our society. A chorus of "amens" would come from all over the church. Encouraged, the pastor would spend much time berating the ugly sin of homosexuality. Tommy Bob hated himself for being such an evil person. There were a lot of things he did not understand, but one thing was clear, this was a secret ... one so deep and so dark that no one must ever find out.

Chapter Four

The show was about to begin. The overhead lights dimmed in the auditorium. Floodlights beamed bright and colorful hues shimmered in the dark. The musicians were the first to come out on the stage, running and skipping to their places. Next, the singers marched to their microphones in single file dressed in identical costumes, white shoes and pants with pale green shirts. The theater was completely filled; some people stood along the outer walls, chairs quickly appeared to seat a few hundred more in the aisles.

The huge speakers at the front of the stage discharged such a powerful blast of music that the vibrations bombarded the audience before their ears had a chance to convert the sound waves into music.

It was a strong beat: electric guitars, drums, keyboards, horns, and a string section all joined in. The worship leader, his long hair pulled back into a ponytail, with his shirt unbuttoned showing off several bulky gold chains around his neck, pointed to the musicians. They began to play. He moved across the stage in exaggerated, step-like motions as if he were tiptoeing through a minefield.

He stopped at the front edge and began to raise and lower his arms in a gigantic arch, looking much like he was trying to fly. Bringing his hands together at the top of the arch, his body swayed in perfect rhythm to the music.

The leader wore a headset that covered only one ear with a microphone contoured to fit close to his mouth. Every sound seemed amplified a thousand times. "Get up on your feet, put your hands together, and let's worship Jesus," he shouted. Immediately more than twelve thousand people leapt to their feet and began shouting. For the next hour, people sang, clapped, danced, cried, and swayed to the music.

Tommy Bob and his parents quickly joined the other worshippers. Shirley had tears running down her heavily powdered cheeks, mascara smearing under her eyes. She stood with her hands out-stretched, a small white handkerchief clutched in her right hand, eyes closed, lips moving.

Thomas Senior raised both arms high, moving to the beat, a look of utter contentment on his handsome face.

Tommy Bob stood between his parents, hands weary of waving hung at his side. His head bowed in a pensive, prayer position.

Like magic, after more than an hour of constant noise, the entire auditorium went quiet. No one directed the people to be silent; it was as if everyone ran out of gas at the same moment. A beautiful, holy hush fell like a mantle over the vast crowd. After a few seconds of complete silence, a deep and booming voice came over the speaker system.

"Ladies and gentlemen. Tulsa is honored to have the finest evangelist on the face of the earth here for five nights of meetings. He has led millions of people to Jesus from every nation of the world. He has authored seventeen books, released more than two-dozen albums and is a well-known celebrity on television. Each evening these services will be broadcast by Tiltun Television around the world."

The voice sounded very much like it was announcing a world-championship boxing match. The hired mouth stretched and annunciated each word in a singsong cadence.

"And now, for the moment you've all been waiting for. Ladies and gentlemen please give a very warm Tulsa welcome for," there was a slight pause as the announcer sucked in enough air to carry him through the forthcoming verbal gymnastics. The voice could have easily just said, "Please welcome T. Tucker Tiltun." But he was not paid a great deal of money to say things normally. It was his job to get the crowd energized, to give the impression that something truly amazing and wonderful was about to happen.

The voice came back high pitched and powerful. For the next sixty seconds the announcer stretched the name like a rubber band, undulating his voice over nearly an octave of range and then at the end slid down the scale to a soft verbal landing.

The crowd was shouting and clapping; the musicians were playing random chords working their way toward a crescendo that would coincide with the pronouncement of the main attraction's last name.

The lights began to flash on and off; a kaleidoscope of colors circled the stage. The orchestra now went into a well-rehearsed musical set that got the entire auditorium swaying, clapping to the beat, looking up expectantly. From off-stage, a beautiful high-pitched voice harmonized perfectly with the orchestra. As rehearsed, the music slowly faded and the only sound left was a single note from a single voice. The sound was vocal purity seldom heard, the audience fell silent; no one moved. The voice held twelve thousand souls breathless, completely spellbound.

Tommy Bob could have sworn T. Tucker Tiltun floated onto the stage. His entrance was so smooth, so well timed and choreographed the crowd did not notice how he came to stand front and center. He just appeared.

He held a microphone close to his glossy lips, but not too close. He did not want to smear his light-red lip liner. The white Armani suit hung in perfect harmony with gravity and was meticulously tailored. The white zip-up boots were new out of the box. The pure powder-puff blue silk shirt and matching tie highlighted his handsome features.

T. Tucker was a gorgeous creature. He was not particularly tall or powerfully built, but his face was remarkable, perfectly symmetrical. His hair was thick, dark, and shiny. It had a slight, natural curl that pushed its way out from the head forming a natural crown of hair. A lock of hair had been pulled forward and sprayed into place forming a flopping curl over his right eye.

Thomas Senior thought to himself, "Hell, T. Tucker probably spent more time at the beauty shop today than Shirley." Eyebrow liner generously applied highlighted his nearly flawless brow. T. Tucker didn't think the liner was necessary, but his make-up artist insisted.

His clear blue eyes contrasted wonderfully with his dark hair. He had not a blemish or a wrinkle. His teeth were straight and white. There was no doubt, when God created T. Tucker, he created a gorgeous human being.

For the next sixty minutes T. Tucker sang, danced, laughed, and wept big crocodile tears that ran freely down his cheeks. He made no effort to wipe them away; he seemed to wear them as a badge of compassion. The women loved his sensitivity.

Even Shirley thought she felt some strange long-forgotten feeling of arousal; T. Tucker was so sexually attractive. Fortunately the drugs made her feelings a fleeting blur as one emotion ran easily into the next in a confused, happy state of sedation.

The show was all masterfully staged. His storytelling was flawless. He mixed his singing and monologues with exceptional skill; story flowed into song and song flowed into story. From the first note the participants were willing captives to T. Tucker's charms. Just before the offering he told stories of starving and suffering children in Africa. Using his oratory magic he painted a word-picture of the suffering, abandon, starving, hopeless children. "Here's a song I wrote for the children," he said and slipped into a song he had written. Halfway through the song there was a rustling sound in the auditorium, like the fall wind blowing among the Aspen trees, as men reached for their wallets and women opened their purses, looking for their check books.

The ushers had been trained well; they appeared on cue and began passing the baskets. These were no ordinary baskets. T. Tucker Tiltun Ministries had them custom designed and handmade in Mexico. They were the size of small washtubs, but much deeper. Years of experience showed that it was not uncommon for people to be so overwhelmed by his story and song that they would empty their pockets, turn their purses upside down, and dump the entire contents into the baskets. In the story or song, T. Tucker casually mentioned that jewelry, watches, and anything of value could be converted to cash. "Remember the poor children," he crooned.

The baskets filled quickly, keeping the back-up ushers on their toes making sure that empty baskets were always on hand. The full ones were taken to the security office and dumped into thirty-five gallon bins to be sorted through later. Once emptied, the baskets returned to active duty to be filled again and again. On a good night, in a wealthy city like Tulsa, a one-hundred-thousand dollar offering was not unusual. T. Tucker Tiltun Ministries only scheduled wealthy cities.

Near the end of the show, T. Tucker gave an emotional appeal for those who did not know Jesus to come forward. If there were sick, emotionally distressed, anyone with financial or marital needs, all should come forward. He assured them that trained counselors would be there to help.

He also mentioned that his books would be for sale at the bookstall. There were also T-shirts, caps, coffee cups, and other memorabilia, but T. Tucker did not mention that from the stage.

Nearly twenty-five hundred people pushed forward during his last song, and as the counselors came in from a special door at the side of the auditorium, cards were distributed and names and addresses collected for T. Tucker's mailing list.

By the time T. Tucker finished, he was drenched in sweat, his beautiful five-thousand-dollar suit baptized in perspiration clung to his body. Two of his personal assistants met him as he left the stage and escorted him to the VIP dressing rooms. He fell exhausted into a chair and took a long drink from a glass of Perrier. After resting for nearly twenty minutes, with a towel over his face, he went into the bathroom for a hot shower.

Thomas looked at his watch. It was ten-twenty. People were still packed in the front. He, Shirley, and Tommy Bob were blocked from leaving by the throng of seekers. He was in no particular hurry, though. Tammy Sue would be waiting. Thomas felt a hand on his shoulder. Someone had come up from behind; he turned to see who it was.

"Excuse me, Mr. Asbury, my name is Steve. I work for Tiltun Ministries. Mr. Tiltun asked if it would be possible for you and your family to join him in his dressing room for a few minutes? He sends this request personally."

Thomas had been an early financial supporter of T. Tucker and although they were not genuine friends, they were respectful toward one another. Thomas respected anyone who made more money than he did.

"Why sure," he replied without consulting Shirley. "Tell T. Tucker that we will stop by for a few minutes."

The dressing room at the Piedmont had changed since Thomas' last visit three years prior. With Tulsa on the main touring circuit for rock bands and stage shows, the dressing room now looked more like a five-star hotel suite than a place backstage to change costumes.

Steve was there to meet them as they reached the door. He quickly ushered them in and shut the door behind them, giving the security guard a stern look which meant no disturbances. There were more than fifty people, mostly young women waiting in the hallway to catch a glimpse of T. Tucker.

The itinerant evangelist was standing at a small table looking over the food that was magnificently arranged on it. He was dressed casually, a pair of khaki pants and a black polo shirt, his feet in a pair of penny-loafers, no socks. Shirley thought he looked more handsome in this casual attire than he did onstage. His dark, thick hair was still damp; you could still see the brush tracks along the sides.

"Well, Thomas, what a pleasure to see you." He walked over and extended his hand, putting the other hand gently on Thomas' shoulder. He smiled and said, "I saw you sitting up front, I see my people took good care of you." Thomas said nothing but did smile back.

"Shirley, my goodness do you look lovely tonight! You are just as gorgeous as ever." His voice full of sincerity, he sounded like he really meant it. He kissed her lightly on the cheek.

Shirley wanted to respond. There was something deep within that beckoned her to throw her arms around his neck and kiss him back; but in her current state of drug intoxication, her brain and her body were not connecting very well so she just squeezed his hand and pretended to be shy instead of stoned.

"Tucker you are a lying fool, but I love you anyway," she said as she turned to take off her jacket. Steve moved expertly behind her, effortlessly removing the jacket and hanging it by the door.

"Who in the world is this fine-looking young man?" T. Tucker walked over to Tommy Bob and put his hand on his shoulder. He had to look up slightly as Tommy Bob was a couple of inches taller. "This can't possibly be Tommy Bob. Why the last time I saw him, he was only this high," he chuckled, holding his right hand at the level of his waist.

Tommy Bob felt uncomfortable. Close range attention from an adult, especially someone as famous and powerful as T. Tucker, made him feel uncomfortable. He wanted to get away. But at the same time there was a strong attraction, like a magnet pulling steel.

"Ya'll come over and try some of this food." Tommy Bob noticed that T. Tucker's polished English was gone and he was now speaking with a slight southern twang. He also noticed how incredibly handsome and appealing T. Tucker was. No question, he was the most beautiful man Tommy had ever seen.

After thirty minutes of chatting about mutual friends and catching up on the latest personal news, Thomas looked at his watch and suggested it was time for them to go. He knew that Tammy Sue, a stripper at one of the bars on the south side and his latest love interest, would wait for him for a while; but if he did not show up soon she would just as likely go out partying with the highest bidder. There were always men waiting after her performance.

The Asbury family made their way to the door. Steve was there to help Shirley put on her jacket. They had said their goodbyes and had just turned to walk out the door when T. Tucker said rather casually, "Tommy Bob, did you enjoy the service tonight?"

Tommy Bob was caught off guard. T. Tucker had not spoken directly to him at all during the time they were together, but he answered clearly. "Yes sir, I thought it was exceptional." His blue eyes made contact with T. Tucker's blue eyes and there was a sudden burst of electricity within Tommy Bob's head. He thought for sure everyone in the room had noticed it, but Shirley and Thomas showed no signs.

"Well perhaps you'd like to come back tomorrow night and see how this all works from behind the stage. You would be my special guest, if that is okay with your folks." His voice trailed off as his eyes turned to Thomas and then Shirley.

By now Shirley wasn't doing so well. She was starting to slur her words and was drooling very slightly from the right corner of her mouth. The words of T. Tucker's question were still bouncing around in her head trying to land on a working brain cell, when Thomas answered for them both.

Thomas glanced yet again at his watch; he wanted to get out the door. "Oh, sure I think it would be fine for Tommy Bob to come back tomorrow, if you want to, that is." He said looking at his son.

"Yes, sir, that would be wonderful." Tommy Bob flashed the brightest smile his father had seen in months.

"Great, I'll have my driver come by for you. Steve make sure someone calls and gets directions. I think you have moved since I was last at your house. You don't still live on South Jamestone do you?"

T. Tucker seemed to enjoy delaying the now-fidgeting Thomas. T. Tucker knew he could not possibly be that anxious just to go home to be with his darling wife.

Tommy Bob went back every night for the next four nights. The second evening he was T. Tucker's guest; from then on he was his lover.

* *

The Asbury's had never seen their son so happy. His grades remained excellent, he continued playing sports at school, and he had made some new friends. For more than a year and a half, about every three months, T. Tucker would send his private jet to pick up Tommy Bob and bring him to his services. His mother was so proud of him for wanting to be around Christian men, especially a respected and famous man like T. Tucker.

After Tommy Bob graduated from high school, the invitations from T. Tucker slowed and then stopped. Tommy Bob was not angry or hurt; he was growing tired of all the hype and fanfare surrounding T. Tucker. He was ready to move on with his life. His parents had insisted he attend a Christian college; they chose a conservative school in Dallas.

Tommy Bob loved learning at the collegiate level. He was no longer treated like a child but instead as a thinking adult. His professors were learned men who seemed to know the answer to every question. There was an unspoken fervor that drove the professors, a passion that came from knowing they were right and all others were wrong. This consuming fire of narrow legalism was contagious. Tommy Bob's long wandering in the forest of confusion and self-doubt was coming to a glorious end.

Chapter Five
Asyut, Egypt 1985

There were fifteen orphanages in Egypt, all run by the Department of Human Services. This one was Number Seven. Located on the outskirts of Asyut, it had once been a hospital for leprosy patients. Built more than fifty years ago, the two beige buildings showed the effects of the hot sun and blasting wind. The smaller structure housed administration and the larger two-story building in back housed the children. The maximum capacity set by the government was fifty orphans. There were currently eighty-three. No one ever bothered checking the actual numbers.

Fatima was the director; she had always been the director. Her office was on the left, at the far end of the dark hallway that led from the main entrance. It could have been any government office in the country; they all looked the same, faded hospital-green walls, a light gray metal desk with matching file cabinet, and a ceiling fan with one crooked blade.

A picture of the President hung on the wall behind her desk. Someone had bumped it once long ago, and it hung to one side making it look like the President could slide from his chair at any moment. A small black and white television sat on an up-turned wooden crate. Fatima never missed her favorite afternoon TV dramas.

Fatima was the perfect bureaucrat. She realized early on that running an orphanage was not about human compassion; it was not about the children; it was not about some great moral issue of children's rights or their needs. It was simply a function of the state. Her cousin, a lifelong government bureaucrat himself, had appointed her as the director. As long as she filled out the correct paperwork and made sure the forms were delivered to the proper authority on time and did not deviate from the policy manual or cause any problems, her job was secured. She had burrowed her way so deeply into the system that no one questioned or cared much what see did.

In the early years she actually cared for the children brought to her,

30

but emotionally it was too overwhelming. Half of the babies carried through the front door would not live to see their first birthday. If they did survive, many were mentally or physically handicapped because of nutritional deprivation.

Orphanage Number Seven was the intake port for the national orphanage system; children from birth to five years old started here. If they reached six years old, they were sent to orphanage Number One in the Cairo. There, a weak attempt was made at educating the kids and finally, they were spit out of the system at sixteen. Most ended up on the streets; adoption is rare.

Fatima looked at her watch, only thirty minutes before she could lock her office door and head home. She was watching a soap opera on the small television with one of her assistants. The phone on her desk rang, her assistant picked it up and listened for a moment, then hung up.

"We have a new arrival," she said with no emotion.

Fatima looked again at her watch, "It never fails. Why do these people wait until I am just about to go out the door to bring in these babies?" she said to no one in particular.

To complete the initial paperwork and get the child in the system would take at least an hour; she would miss her bus. Fortunately, two babies had died within the past week so there was space. By putting two or three babies to a bed, Fatima had a lot of leeway for accepting new infants. Turning them down required more paperwork than accepting them.

Fatima reached for the second drawer on the right side of her desk and opened it roughly. She pulled out a thick, well-worn registry, plopped it on her desk, and began flipping the pages till she came to the last entry.

A worker dressed in an ill-fitting, stained, light-blue uniform appeared in the doorway carrying a small bundle. Fatima looked up. "At least this one arrived wrapped in something," she thought to herself. She had seen them arrive naked in cardboard boxes, wrapped in leaves; one was brought in a paper bag. At least this one had a pale yellow and gray flowered bit of cloth covering it. "Looks like a piece of an old sheet," Fatima said to the girl holding the child. "What do we have?" Fatima asked quickly.

"A boy, maybe three or four days old" replied the worker, looking down at the baby.

"A boy, that is pretty unusual," Fatima thought. Eight out of ten babies brought to the orphanage were girls. It was not unusual for a friend or neighbor to take in the boys; they made good workers and had some value, but girls were worthless. "I don't know why these women don't have an abortion and save everyone a lot of trouble," Fatima said as she pushed her chair back from the desk.

Fatima stood up and walked around the corner of her desk. She pushed her oversized glasses back to the bridge of her nose and with empty eyes looked into the baby's face. It was not unusual for people to keep the babies for a few days, weeks, or even months to see if they could use them in some way. If they couldn't, they'd bring them in. Rarely did mothers bring the babies. It was usually family or friends or neighbors who did the dirty work.

There was one part of the process that Fatima particularly disliked, the naming. She had tried different techniques over the years. It seemed to be such a meaningless step; better to just tattoo a number on their butt — easier to track and a lot less effort. However, the bureaucrats required a name, actually two, so several years ago she devised her own clever method.

She found an old book of babies' names; for each day of the week she listed five given or first names and three surnames. In Egypt, the child is given their first name and then takes the name of their father for the second name and the name of the grandfather for a third. There are no family names as such. Because this information was not known for the babies dropped off at the orphanage, Fatima had to make it up. She chose three American presidents' surnames: Washington, Roosevelt, and Jefferson.

The book of names was printed in the United States, so all the suggested first names were Western. It proved to be a good way to monitor kids coming through her program. No other children in the country had the distinctive Western names her kids did, so if one of "her" children ever did anything important or significant, she could of course take some credit. After twenty-five years, none had done anything notable that she knew of ... but who knows?

Fatima looked at the wrinkled, tea-stained, government-issued calendar on her desk. Today was Tuesday. She consulted her list and randomly put her pen on a name: Simon. She moved her hand over to the right and picked a surname: Roosevelt. Her simple invention made it so much easier, completely random and objective, very little effort.

She finished the paperwork in forty-five minutes, closed the registry, and returned it to its proper place. Fatima glanced at her watch; ten minutes to catch the bus three blocks away. Putting her over-loaded body into high gear, she flung her purse over her shoulder, pulled the plug on the TV, turned off the crooked-bladed fan, closed the door, and locked it with a key hung around her neck. Hurriedly she shuffled down the hall and out the front door.

The baby, Simon Roosevelt, was taken to room six and placed on a bed between two other babies. Simon threw his tiny fists about wildly, kicked his legs, and filled his new lungs with enough air to let out a wail of fear and anger. The worker ignored his pleas; she placed a piece of tape on the wall over his head, looked at the piece of paper carried on a clip-board, and wrote his name with red ink on the tape. It was someone else's job to feed him and change his dirty diapers in two or three hours. She closed the door and walked down the dimly-lit hall. Simon's fate was sealed.

Asyut, Upper Egypt
Hartford School for Girls, 1985

Victoria Lovejoy received a note from the director of the school. The gate-keeper, his dirty white turban showing signs of perspiration seeping through, gave it to her on her way back from morning tea. Asyut is a hot place; summer temperatures easily reach one hundred twenty degrees. It is the principle city for upper Egypt, the region south of Cairo to the Sudan border.

Presbyterian missionaries founded the Hartford School for Girls in 1925. The school was intended to be a place for missionaries working in remote parts of Africa to send their children for schooling. By the late 1960's most missionaries were gone and the facilities were empty. The Presbyterian Church gave the property to another nonprofit organization based in England. They reopened the Hartford School for Girls.

In this part of Egypt, having a son was an occasion of great joy. They were perceived as valuable, productive property. Having a daughter was not a joyous occasion. Many families would keep the daughters if they could. But if times got hard, as they often did, the girls would be turned out of the family, left to fend for themselves. Or they would be sold to traders and end up as prostitutes in Beirut or Nicosia or some other Middle Eastern city. Hartford was the only lifeline for the forty girls residing there. The girls were taught English, given the equivalent of a high school education, and taught a trade.

The compound was small, surrounded by high red-brick walls. Four large buildings, one on each side of the compound, formed a lovely court-yard in the middle. The missionaries had tended the gardens well and they were one of the few beautiful places in all of Asyut. Victoria stood in the shade of the courtyard and opened the note. "Please be in my office at eleven this morning. Mr. Tadburn." Victoria arrived a few min-utes early and waited. At the Hartford School for Girls, being tardy is simply not acceptable. Precisely at eleven o'clock Mr. Tadburn opened his office door and motioned for her to come in.

"We have a new arrival scheduled for today," Mr. Tadburn said as he walked behind his desk and sat down. "She will be assigned to you. I do not know much about her. You can read her file if you like. I know it is a bit unusual to take someone after the school term has begun, but we do have one space available, so I have decided to accept her. Her name is Rebekah Ibrahim; she comes from one of the villages up river." He looked up at Victoria, still standing.

His bald head shined with perspiration. "Maybe if he did not wear a coat, shirt, and tie every day in this heat he would not sweat so much," Victoria thought to herself. Mr. Tadburn handed her the file. "When will she be arriving?" Victoria asked.

"Sometime this afternoon, I will let you know when she gets here." He reached for another file. The meeting was over.

Victoria went back to her small flat above the dorm rooms. She sat down and read the one-page application. It told her nothing really. She knew from her many years as a houseparent that only a face-to-face meeting with Rebekah would give her a sense of what was in store. One thing for certain, the girl would tell a sad story. They all did.

About half past two, Victoria was walking across the courtyard to pick up her mail. As she passed by the office building, she noticed an elderly woman and a young girl trudging up the walk. They had just entered the compound through the white front gate.

Victoria stopped and waited until they came to her. The lanky young girl walked dejectedly two paces behind an old lady Victoria took to be the grandmother. The older woman walked briskly like she was in a hurry. The girl's shoulders stooped forward, her long, thick hair hid her face. She took elongated steps bouncing a plastic bag off her right knee, and she carried a small, battered, pink plastic suitcase in her left hand. The girl was tall, taller than Victoria. Victoria noticed the girl had on a pair of dirty, clear plastic sandals at least two sizes too large. They were worn and tattered and split just above the big toe. Her faded and torn dress hung on her slender frame like a towel thrown carelessly over a rack.

The older woman seemed nervous and uncomfortable. After Victoria greeted them and introduced herself, the woman with Rebekah turned to leave.

"Would you like to have a cup of tea and see the place before you go?" Victoria asked.

"No, I must be going," she said.

The woman started once again to leave, but paused. She turned her wrinkled, angry face back to Rebekah. "Good luck to you, child. Try and make something of yourself." She turned and walked quickly down the path and out the gate. No farewell, no second glance over her shoulder, she scurried across the street like a rat fleeing daylight and disappeared around the corner.

Rebekah stood in front of Miss Lovejoy, not looking up. Victoria gently reached out and put her hand on Rebekah's stooped shoulder. Rebekah stiffened under the thin dress.

"Rebekah, don't be afraid. I know life looks pretty grim at the moment, but we will get through this, you wait and see." This was the fall of 1985. Rebekah was fourteen.

Rebekah remembered very little of her first days at Hartford. The directors were from England, most of the teaching staff were foreigners with a few locals working in the compound. Her memory of meeting Miss Lovejoy in the garden on the first day stayed with her. She had been so afraid and sad and felt so alone; Miss Lovejoy's touch sent shivers down her back.

Her first impression of her new "parent" was not very positive. Miss Lovejoy was short, overweight, with thinning gray hair. Her glasses sat perched on the end of her pug nose, until shoved back into place. The sliding started again immediately. Behind the glasses the hazel eyes were oversized, like headlights on a car. Rebekah dreaded having Miss Lovejoy as a houseparent.

Miss Lovejoy had six girls to care for, and care she did. A no-nonsense, strict disciplinarian, Victoria was firm but kind. Victoria spoke Arabic well, accented but clear. She was always there to encourage, instruct, correct, and pray for her girls. In time, Rebekah responded to such love like a flower to sunshine and returned her love easily to Victoria.

Rebekah's clearest memories were of Miss Lovejoy holding her tight at night as she wept for her real mother and sitting with her through the dark hours when the nightmares started. Rebekah could never tell Victoria the whole story. She simply said she was sent away from her family because they had too many children and could not afford to have her around. Victoria did not completely believe her account, but it was not uncommon for families in upper Egypt to send children away. Still, Victoria thought Rebekah's eyes told a deeper and far more painful tale.

Chapter Six

"I am an old lady," Victoria mused one day while listening to Rebekah chat as she did her homework. Rebekah was talking non-stop about her day. "The first forty-two years of my life wasted, the last twenty years very fulfilling," thought Victoria. She was referring to her earlier life as a hopeless alcoholic. Victoria had been sober for nearly twenty-one years.

She loved her girls and poured her life into each one. The girls usually responded to love and discipline, not all but a good number. Victoria was proud of the outstanding record her girls had achieved over the years. Many had gone on to excellent professions and some now filled important positions in business and government. She kept in contact with many of her graduates. There was an unspoken "old girls network." If any of her younger girls needed a place to live or a job the older graduates would find a way to help. It gave Victoria great joy to see the girls looking out for one another. No one else would.

Victoria realized Rebekah had stopped speaking. She looked down at the young lady. Miss Lovejoy was sitting in her favorite rocking chair. Rebekah liked sitting on the floor at her feet, working on a small table. Rebekah looked up at her and smiled. "What a special young lady," Victoria thought. Rebekah's black eyes were unusually bright, beautiful, and hinted at an unusual intelligence. But they also occasionally flashed that unmistaken look of sadness, hurt, and anger. Whoever said the eyes were the windows to the soul was profoundly accurate. Almost every girl in the school had a similar look. Victoria could not quite describe it, but she knew the gaze of a wounded heart.

Miss Lovejoy had watched Rebekah struggle. When she arrived, she looked like a frightened, abandoned animal. Victoria knew that a steady hand was necessary for Rebekah to make it through the first months. She purposely set out to guide Rebekah through the first and most difficult phase. Being at Hartford was a unique opportunity; those who got in considered themselves to be fabulously lucky.

And yet it also marked the final act of rejection. There was no going home, no going back. Hartford had a strict policy, once admitted no contact with the family. Too many girls in the early days left to spend time with family and never returned. Rumor had it they ended up being forced into marriage or sold. Each new student must forge a new identity. It was a painful time.

Victoria was aware that those who made it had to make it on their own. She could not do it for them. She could only walk close and offer a stable hand as they mourned the loss.

Rebekah was better than most at hiding her feelings. Victoria knew the pent-up emotions had to come out in some form; she just hoped it would be positive and not destructive.

Rebekah's first year and a half at Hartford had gone well. Academically she excelled, but her emotions were still sealed tight. Victoria told her many simple stories about Jesus. There seemed to be an inner connection. Rebekah asked many questions at first, but slowly the questions subsided. Victoria thought Rebekah had lost interest. Then Rebekah began to give her own insights and thoughts about Jesus. Victoria knew the same love-scarred hand that reached out to her years ago was now gently holding Rebekah's.

Several months later Rebekah sat beside Miss Lovejoy on the courtyard bench. Victoria could tell something was troubling her.

"Why do I still feel so badly inside, Miss Lovejoy? I have prayed and asked Jesus to take the hurt inside, but it is still there. Is there something wrong with me?" Rebekah asked.

Victoria glanced at Rebekah and then spoke in a low gentle voice. "Rebekah, some of the hurt we feel is because people have done things to us that cause the inner pain. Sometimes it's our own mistakes. If we forgive, we don't allow our hearts to become hard and bitter. If we face truthfully the issues, then time will help heal the hurt."

Victoria turned and looked full into Rebekah's face. "But there is also another aspect to our pain. Rebekah, I am going to tell you something you may not fully understand now. Maybe as you grow older you will comprehend it better. I am sixty-three years old and still do not have much understanding."

Miss Lovejoy shifted her position so she could see Rebekah a bit better. "I can only tell you what I have experienced, Rebekah. It may not be completely true, but it does have some application to all of us women. I think there is some sort of giant bucket of universal pain. When females are born, each one must take a portion of it. It is our burden to carry in this life. It is the weight of womanhood, the agony of the soul is the only way I know how to describe it."

"Does knowing Jesus make it any easier?" Rebekah asked softly.

There was a very long pause. Victoria took off her glasses and rubbed her oversized eyes. She seemed to be stalling. Finally, putting her glasses back on, she pushed them tight against her nose and answered, "To be honest, Rebekah, no. Not easier, but bearable. He gives us a sense of destiny. In some way, it might be joining Him in the eternal agony for man, and by doing so there is a greater cause than just our own despair. The spirit of mourning that every woman carries may be God's way of sharing the pain He feels over the lost state of man." Victoria said, not very convincingly.

"That is not very good news," Rebekah responded.

"Rebekah, I will not try and make something seem better than it is," Victoria continued. "It is far more noble to look truth straight in the eye and embrace it — even though it is not pleasant — than to wrap our arms around untruth, just to make ourselves more comfortable." Victoria rocked back in her chair.

This kind of honest talk with Rebekah continued over the next years. Rebekah had many questions and Miss Lovejoy gave her best answers; maybe not always the correct ones, but the best she had. At times Rebekah responded positively; she seemed to understand. Other times she would become sullen and remote, pulling back from Miss Lovejoy and the other students. Victoria knew Rebekah was still in the balance, her prayers for Rebekah intensified. She had seen too many girls come to this same point and then slip back, swallowed in despair and bitterness.

Chapter Seven

Miss Lovejoy sat in the garden waiting for Rebekah to arrive home from school. Rebekah had done so well in her English class, she now attended some advanced classes at a private institute in town. Victoria paid for them herself. She heard Rebekah before she saw her. Rebekah was shouting to a friend across the road. She opened the gate and walked toward the building where the girls lived; she did not see Victoria waiting for her.

Victoria noticed how much Rebekah had grown. She was now an extraordinarily beautiful young lady. Victoria loved Rebekah as her own child. The most difficult part of her job was saying goodbye. Her girls would come and they would go. Every time one left, Victoria felt the loss. But like a tree that is pruned each autumn gets stronger and more productive, Victoria felt that she had more love to give to the next girl.

"Rebekah!" Miss Lovejoy called.

"Miss Lovejoy, I am sorry. I did not see you sitting there." Rebekah walked over and gave Miss Lovejoy a kiss on the cheek and sat down beside her. Rebekah put her elbows on her knees and placed her lovely chin in her hands. She stared at the ground.

After a few moments Victoria asked, "You look deep in thought, my dear. What are you thinking about?"

"I take my final examinations in three weeks. I'm so nervous and scared. I'm afraid I will not do very well," Rebekah responded.

"You listen to me, Rebekah. I have been working with students for more than forty years; you are one of the brightest and best students I have ever seen. You are not just intelligent, but you work hard — a rare combination. I know you will do just fine." Miss Lovejoy turned her head and coughed a deep, lung-cleansing cough. But it didn't stop.

"Are you all right Miss Lovejoy?" Rebekah asked with fear in her voice.

"Oh, I am fine. Just a bad cough," Victoria lied.

Rebekah did very well on her exams and was accepted to university. Victoria, however, grew increasingly ill and weak. The last time Rebekah saw her was the day she left for university. Miss Lovejoy was standing in the garden. She had bought Rebekah a beautiful new tan-colored leather suitcase. Rebekah carried it proudly to where the small black and white taxi waited. Victoria walked over to where Rebekah stood; she took long slow breaths, each one a struggle.

Rebekah stood five inches taller than Miss Lovejoy, so Victoria had to reach up with both her trembling hands. She put one on each side of Rebekah's neck and pulled her face close to her own.

Rebekah saw that illness and age were overtaking her beloved mother, confidante, and friend. As she looked into the eyes of love, she saw the pure, burning fire of devotion shining through. Rebekah knew she was loved; Victoria's eyes told the truth.

Speaking softly, Victoria said to Rebekah, "Rebekah, my dear child, I have loved you with my whole heart. It is time now for you to go on to the next stage of your life's journey. It is so very painful to say our goodbyes, but unless we bid farewell to one season of our lives we cannot greet the next. You must get used to letting go. Life is full of coming and going. I shall always love you and pray for you. I want you to know how very proud I am of you. You must promise to help the other girls when you can. Always keep a hand outstretched to others. I love you, Rebekah."

Rebekah was sobbing. She reached down to embrace the most beautiful woman in the world. She clung to Victoria as long as she could, but the taxi driver was glaring as he stood next to the open door. It was time to go. Victoria walked to the gate and turned to wave a final farewell. As the taxi departed, Victoria doubled over as the violent onset of uncontrolled coughing began once again. Her darling Rebekah was gone; Victoria was not certain which was more painful, the burning in her lungs or the ache in her heart.

Rebekah attended the American University of Cairo, a six-hour train ride from Asyut. At the end of her first year at university Rebekah received a call from one of the girls that had been at Hartford with her. Through the sobs she said Miss Lovejoy had died. Two weeks later, a small package arrived from Hartford School for Girls. In it was a note stating that Miss Lovejoy had left specific instructions that these items be sent to Rebekah.

Rebekah placed the box reverently on the table. Her hands trembled as she cut the string holding the box closed. Pulling back the flaps of the small carton she saw Miss Lovejoy's Bible and a tiny white jewelry box. The smaller box contained a ring and a silver necklace that Miss Lovejoy always wore.

Rebekah wept bitterly as she grieved the loss of her "mother." That is what Victoria Lovejoy was to Rebekah: a beautiful, kind, wise mother. Once again, Rebekah was alone. The frantic sense of being abandoned gripped her soul and fear flooded her mind. What would she ever do now that the one person who believed so strongly in her was gone? "I mustn't let Miss Lovejoy down. I mustn't disappoint her. I will survive and I will make something of my life," Rebekah vowed as salty tears dripped from her chin on to Miss Lovejoy's worn and tattered Bible.

Chapter Eight

Tommy Bob graduated from Faith College in 1988, top in his class and student body president. His collegiate days were a good time for him to grow up. He intentionally put some emotional distance between himself and his overbearing, hard-driving father and his pathetic, weak, drug-controlled mother. He detested them both but for different reasons. His own life was progressing quite well.

His teachers in college were good men: humorless men, with pinched faces and very tight sphincter muscles, but men who had to be this way because they were guarding God's truth from an evil society. For Tommy Bob the line separating right and wrong, good and bad, sin and righteousness was getting so incredibly clear. The more he threw himself into his fanatic belief system, the better he felt about himself. He was doing the right thing and God would love him for that. And the more fanatical he became, the more God would be pleased with him. It was so simple. All the correct answers were being given to him, precept upon precept, Scripture by Scripture. He wasn't encouraged to think independently for himself; he only needed to memorize the truth and regurgitate on demand.

About every three months or so the homosexual urgings would get too strong to resist. He told his friends he was going home for the weekend. Instead, he would head into Dallas' sleazy district. He would spend the two days in gay bars and his gay friends' homes. They had no idea who he was or where he came from; they didn't care.

During his college years, Tommy Bob carefully and slowly pieced together the needed rationale for his sexual behavior. If God was truly all-knowing and all-powerful and had predetermined the smallest choice of man, then whatever happened was part of God's plan from the beginning. So all choices at one level are good. What mattered most was trying to obey the commands of Christ. No one could ever keep them entirely, everyone was bound to fail at some point, and his point of preordained failure was his homosexuality. For others it might be greed, power, or pride. But it was all covered by the death of Christ, part of God's eternal plan. It was the effort, the striving to do right wherein true virtue was hidden.

Tommy Bob adopted a standard of holiness so high, so rigid, so impossible that no one could live up to it. Not even himself, but he tried to. His classmates thought he was the most holy, righteous man they knew. Even some of his professors where impressed with his fervor. In his mind, the fact that he had this high standard for himself meant he could impose it on others and judge others by it. This gave him a wonderful sense of superiority and aloofness. It also kept people from getting too close to his own little secret.

In September of 1988, Tommy Bob began his formal seminary training at Dallas Southern School of Theology. His status as the most conservative, best-looking, brightest, most-articulate, wealthiest student the seminary had seen in quite some time, drew attention. The Dean encouraged him to pursue a doctorate degree. It added another two years on to his seminary time, but Thomas was in no hurry.

Upon completing his doctorate the seminary leaders recommended Tommy Bob be placed on a fast track for leadership in the denomination. After much discussion at the headquarters, they gave him an offer to be an associate pastor at a large and wealthy church in North Chicago. Headquarters knew the senior pastor was going to retire in two to three years and they wanted Tommy Bob postured to take his place.

The Reverend Jefferson Crockett, president of the Conservative Evangelical Baptist Union, requested a meeting with Tommy Bob. He made two recommendations — actually they were more than suggestions. If he wanted the job as associate pastor at North Heights Baptist in Chicago, he must do two things, first change his name.

"Up north, folks do not trust men with two first names. It sounds too much like some buck-toothed hillbilly," Reverend Crockett said sternly.

Reverend Crockett paused for a brief moment, collecting his thoughts. "The second thing is you need a wife. I've seen too many good young men go into a high-profile position like this and get in trouble with women. So I want you married within the year. And don't go thinking you need to find some beautiful girl and fall in love and all that nonsense. This is a career move. My advice is to get one that is docile and of low intelligence. Make sure she has no aspirations to get involved in your ministry. She is there to have children and take care of the home, nothing more."

As an afterthought Dr. Crockett added, "It is important she is pleasing to your eye. She has got to keep your interest over the years; otherwise you may want to go looking where you shouldn't be looking. Is that clear?"

"Yes, sir," Tommy Bob said. He walked out the door and went straight into the restroom. He thought he was going to throw up. He had never considered marriage before; he somehow thought that he could go through the rest of his life as he went through seminary. He was very good at hiding what he did.

Chapter Nine

The move to Chicago proved a difficult time for Dr. Thomas Asbury, as he was now known. The church was large; nearly five thousand filled the sanctuary on any Sunday morning. Many wealthy and influential people of Chicago's society attended. Thomas knew he would have to guard his secret more closely than ever. He could no longer go openly to the gay bars. He snuck into a few during his first months in Chicago, but thought he recognized one of the deacons from the church and panicked.

It scared him so badly he decided it was time to find a wife. It might be helpful to be married; it never hurt to have another layer of cover when you are hiding a forbidden secret. With some serious effort, Thomas identified nearly a dozen women that fit the Reverend Crockett's criteria. Further investigation narrowed the field to three. He finally picked one.

Thomas developed a narrowing pattern in his thinking. Some thought it unlikely or even impossible, but he was becoming more and more conservative theologically. His dark side had to be shielded at all costs. To compensate for the fear and insecurity the darkness generated, Thomas wore an air of superiority. Inwardly he hated the weak souls who did not measure up to his standards. He treated them with hostility and intellectual contempt. Given his high moral ground, people would never think to suspect his behavior. He loved the feeling of being theologically and morally superior.

The first three years at North Heights were good for Dr. Asbury. He requested that everyone except the senior pastor call him Dr. Asbury. He married Kathy, a pretty but troubled and shy young lady. She worshipped Thomas and thought she was the luckiest girl in the world to marry such a wonderful man. His star was certainly rising among the denominational hierarchy. He was an excellent teacher and a proficient administrator; several influential parishioners were ready to have him as their next senior pastor.

Trouble started, though, when a young boy came to the youth leader to say he was sexually involved with Dr. Asbury. The whole incident was quietly passed on to Reverend Crockett. He flew to Chicago and interviewed the boy, who was twelve and came from a single parent home. Dr. Asbury denied the situation and blamed the boy for having a crush on him. He, of course, was only trying to help the troubled young man.

Dr. Asbury was absolutely outraged that anyone would question his integrity. He demanded an apology. But something of the boy's honesty and innocence convinced Reverend Crockett there was more to the story. But nothing was done. When a second boy came forward two years later with a similar story, Reverend Crockett had no choice but to call an emergency meeting of the denomination's Board of Directors. They flew in from all over the U.S.

"Gentlemen, we have a problem," Reverend Crockett began. He then gave a detailed account of the situation in Chicago. After he had briefed the board members, he opened the meeting for questions.

"Is there any way to keep this quiet?" a businessman from California asked. "If this gets out, we are in deep trouble. We are already facing significant financial challenges and this could hurt us deeply." The other board members nodded in agreement and looked solemnly to Reverend Crockett.

"We have offered money to the boys involved and some counseling, if they agree to sign a written statement stating they had conspired to make up the entire story. Our attorneys advised us this would certainly help later on if further allegations were made," Reverend Crockett announced. "We did promise that Dr. Asbury would be relocated within the next three months."

"Has Dr. Asbury acknowledged any wrong doing?" asked another.

"No, he maintains it is all a mistake. Some kind of plot to destroy his ministry." The discussion took the better part of the morning. They worked hard at what they called damage control; by the end of the morning, they had a plan in place to cover all contingencies.

The afternoon session began with a discussion of what to do with the good Dr. Asbury. The Reverend Crockett suggested that he be assigned to a foreign mission position. The regional director for Egypt had just returned to the United States for health reasons, and they were looking for someone to replace him. Dr. Asbury would be the perfect person.

In closing the emergency meeting, Reverend Crockett took a sip of water from his glass and said, "Thank you, gentlemen, for your help and assistance. Dr. Asbury is the kind of young man we need to one day run this denomination. We can't afford to lose him. We'll put him out of the limelight for awhile and then bring him back. Besides a few years of mission experience will look great on his record." The men sitting around the table all nodded in agreement.

Chapter Ten

Rebekah sat quietly on the beach just outside of Alexandria. The white, silky sand was hot, the sea azure blue, and the sea breeze, fresh and warm, felt good. The three-hour train ride from Cairo was worth it to see the beauty of Alexandria. Sitting next to her was a mother and her three small children. Rebekah watched carefully as the mother kept busy tending to the needs of each child.

The sun climbed higher into the sky and was beating down with great intensity. Rebekah pulled her hat down over her forehead, reached into her bag, and retrieved a book. A small piece of scrap paper poked above the pages indicating where she had left off. Her eyes scanned the first few lines, but her mind began thinking of her own mother. She lowered her book, still open, to her lap and closed her eyes.

Rebekah tried thinking about her own mother. But no feelings came, only emptiness. Instead Miss Lovejoy's face would come into her mind. Her family was gone forever. She could never return; it would only open old hurts and wounds and raise a lot of questions her mother was sure to have buried long ago. She had better face the reality that she was all alone in the world.

What about her own son? If still alive, he would turn fifteen this year. Her mother's cousin saw to it that tracing his whereabouts would be impossible. She had long since died, taking that precious information with her to the grave. At times Rebekah was obsessive about finding her son; once she returned to where she had given birth and asked neighbors, but no one seemed to know anything. At least no one was willing to talk.

Rebekah had no idea if he had been given away or sold to people in the nearby villages as a worker or given to a family in the city. There was always the possibility he had ended up in an orphanage; she just did not know. Rebekah had once thought about going to the orphanages to see if any babies were brought in August of 1985. But then she thought,

"What would I do if I did find him? I have no way to support him and no one to help me. Maybe it's better not to find him." But the fact that she was a mother with a son she did not know remained a constant source of anguish.

Quite randomly Rebekah's thoughts shifted to her university days. After a teary farewell to Miss Lovejoy and some very lonely first months in Cairo, Rebekah discovered she loved the city and the university setting. Cairo, the largest city in Africa with nearly twenty million people, was constantly busy. At two in the morning people would still be out walking the streets, shopping, and going to restaurants. At Hartford she had to be in bed every night at ten. Between studies, her new friends, and her newfound freedom, she was busy day and night. In the busyness, she forgot some of the hurt. She learned early on that work was an excellent way to mask the inner turmoil.

She found a thriving church bursting with university students and young professionals. It was dynamic. The pastor, Mounir Habib was a sixty-year-old balding, overweight, giant of a man. His easy laughter and friendly hugs made everyone feel part of a big family. Many foreigners also attended the Sunday morning service.

Before long Rebekah was leading several youth ministries in the church. People recognized her leadership gifts; it was so natural for her to take charge and get things done. She was an excellent communicator and spoke often in other churches in the city. She joined the youth leadership team, spent many years serving, and eventually leading a ministry to the young professionals. Pastor Habib loved Rebekah and encouraged her leadership.

Rebekah had no idea that the leadership of her denomination was changing. Dr. Thomas Asbury had just arrived from the United States to take over the thirty-five churches that his denomination had started during the past seventy-five years. Because her church was the largest, most-influential church, Dr. Asbury made it his home.

The church officials who welcomed Dr. Asbury and his wife at the airport were very impressed when they saw this handsome couple. No one was told why Dr. Asbury was being sent to Egypt. The previous director's home was painted and cleaned and made ready for the Asburys. But within a few weeks, Dr. Asbury had notified the local leaders that, at his own expense, he wanted to move into Maadi, a suburb on the south side of the city, far from the denomination offices. He needed to have his space from work, he explained. It was the area of the city where most of the ex-patriots lived. Maadi is a very wealthy and exclusive neighborhood.

Dr. Asbury and Kathy found a beautiful villa with a high security wall around the compound. It had a new swimming pool, red clay tennis courts, and a stunning garden. They interviewed several people for the staff positions in their villa. Kathy hired three ladies, one to cook and two to keep the house.

Dr. Asbury hired just one man to be his personal driver; the gardener came with the house. At the time, it seemed a bit unusual to the gardener, but Dr. Asbury insisted he needed an assistant gardener. He specifically instructed him to find a young boy, someone with no family ties.

"Get a street kid. I want to help some poor child who doesn't have much of a chance in life," Dr. Asbury had ordered. "Surely you can find a boy who would like to live in a beautiful place like this." Dr. Asbury reached into his pocket and pulled out a twenty-dollar bill. "Let's be discreet. I will give you twenty dollars a month in addition to your salary if you take care of everything. Do you understand?"

The gardener understood perfectly. No family; no questions. He now needed to find the right boy. He put the twenty-dollar bill in his frayed front pocket, picked up the shovel he was working with, and walked briskly to his small hut by the gate.

Chapter Eleven
Cairo, Orphanage Number One

The government felt it was more economical to have a centralized system whereby all the orphans from ages six to sixteen were housed in one facility. So at the age of six, Simon was put on a bus with nineteen other kids and transported to the capital city where the state had its central orphanage: Orphanage Number One.

More than five hundred children lived in a series of square, cement buildings, each four stories high. Dirt courtyards divided the two rows of housing units. At the north end was a bare field. This was the sports center. It consisted of two ancient poles; each held a basketball rim nailed to a piece of rotting plywood. No nets. The well-used rims hung down at an angle, not straight out like they were commissioned to do. Further out, was a bare dirt field; this was the soccer field. Wooden goals stood at each end. The orphanage was much like living in a controlled ghetto.

The routine never varied. Up at six thirty; twenty minutes for the orphans to wash their faces, brush their teeth, and make their beds. The beds had to be made according to standards. All four corners of the thread bare blankets were tucked under the mattress, the pillow placed exactly in the center toward the head and angled with one of the corners pointed into the air, making it look like a drop of whipped cream had been placed on each bed. There were six children to a room.

By seven o'clock, they stood like silent soldiers in line outside the dining room. When a whistle sounded, the orphans were allowed in. They moved in a single-file line toward one end of the room where large serving windows made quick work of dispensing food. The dining room was crowded and noisy but very well supervised. Adult monitors walked up and down between the tables making sure everyone remained under control. The slightest deviation from the regulations was quickly corrected.

After breakfast, the orphans became students. They made their way quickly to their deteriorating cement classrooms. The walls were empty. For a blackboard, one rectangular portion of the wall had been painted flat black. Forty cheap, well-used desks were squeezed into a room that comfortably held twenty-five. One teacher and two monitors spent the next four hours giving the students basic instruction in reading, writing, fundamental mathematics, and English.

Government statistics showed that ninety-nine percent of the orphans released into society would never move beyond the basic educational level, so a minimum of effort and expense were allocated for academics. More than education, they needed to learn a skill; that was the afternoon program.

The boys had two choices: carpentry or metalworking. The girls had three: sewing, weaving, or cooking. The government overlooked the fact that more than sixty percent of the so-called graduates from the orphanage system would become drug dealers, pimps, prostitutes, thieves, or worse within two years of leaving.

The front entrance to the orphanage faced a busy city street. The wall along this part of the compound was cement for the first three feet, topped with a wrought-iron fence that extended another seven feet high. The wrought-iron was once painted a light green, but now only patches of the paint were still clinging to their original assignment. Time and rust had persuaded the rest to let go.

At the center of this front wall was a large gate, also of wrought iron. It opened to allow delivery trucks and the occasional government inspector in and out. Each afternoon it opened for another reason. Every orphan, within a year of graduation, was assigned a work apprenticeship job in the city. This work assignment was supposed to help the young adults learn a practical skill and assist them in gaining some social skills as well.

Sitting on the cement part of the wall, looking through the wrought-iron bars, was how Simon passed time in the afternoons. It gave him a sense of freedom. He loved watching the people walk by. Few ever looked in his direction. Simon didn't mind. He felt closer to the people just by watching them. He especially liked to watch families as they strolled by. He would try to guess what they were doing, where they were going, who was the oldest; it was an imaginary game he played.

Simon was fifteen years old today. One of the few things that he knew about himself was his birth date. In the first orphanage, Number Seven, they tried celebrating the children's birthdays every year; but here at Orphanage Number One they never even tried. Too many kids. But each year on his birthday he would play another game.

He tried to imagine what his mother had looked like, where she was, what she was doing. Sometimes in this game, she would come to him and say how very sorry she was she had to give him away and how much she really did love him. She would hold him and he would cry. She would then open the iron gates and take him home with her.

This had been his wish for the past eight years. The kids did not talk about it among themselves very often, but each one had the same fantasy. Even though they had food, shelter, education, and clothes, they missed the very thing no government institution could offer: human love.

Sometimes the kids would talk about how they were going to have their own families, with lots of children; how they would take care of them and love them. It gave them something to hope for.

Simon knew he would feel very sad for several days after his dreaming; that is why he tried to limit it to once a year. It was too painful.

"Simon," Simon looked up to see his best friend, Robert, walking toward him on the street. Robert casually put his hands on the wrought iron bars. He was nearly a foot taller than Simon and powerfully built with muscular arms and a thick chest. Robert was only a year and a half older than Simon, but looked and acted like someone in his mid-twenties. Robert was big and powerful and handsome. He had on a new pair of jeans and a fancy white shirt and the newest style of basketball shoes. Robert adjusted the two new, heavy gold chains around his neck. By his appearance, no one would have guessed his previous residence was Orphanage Number One. Before that, Number Seven.

Robert had been out of the orphanage for more than a year. His assigned job was working with a rug merchant. His real job was dealing drugs to the rich kids on the south side of town.

Simon looked one last time at the people on the street and then looked up at his friend. "Haven't seen you for a long time," Simon shifted his position so he could see Robert better.

"I am ready to begin my own operation," Robert said as he moved closer to the railing. "I have been positioning myself for this past year. I have learned enough of the trade and made enough contacts to strike out on my own." Robert lowered his head so that his lifeless eyes looked directly at Simon.

"I need someone I can trust. The only way to survive out here is to be stronger and smarter than the competition. But I have to move now. There is a chance to take over part of the south side territory. The guy who was selling there disappeared." Robert hesitated. Simon felt a cold chill go down his spine. "Word on the street is, he was shot by the police, but it doesn't matter how he disappeared, only THAT he disappeared," he said with no emotion. "What does matter is that I need to move now before someone else steps in."

Robert was a born conniver. From his earliest days, Simon remembered how Robert always had a scheme to use the system to get ahead. When it came time for new clothes to be distributed, Robert volunteered to help sort them. Of course, the best and nicest he kept for himself. As an early teen he was always hungry, so he recruited one of the girls working in the kitchen to be his girlfriend and got as much food as he wanted. He used bribery, flattery, and/or intimidation to get his way.

Robert had a soft spot in his otherwise hard heart for Simon. They had been together from the beginning. When they had been shipped here, they were roommates. Robert was aggressive, Simon shy. Robert was a bully, Simon a peacemaker. Robert was angry and did not mind hurting people to get his way; Simon was tender and did not want to hurt anyone. Robert felt protective of Simon; he knew if he did not cover for him, he would be squashed like a bug. He took his role as self-imposed protector seriously.

"I have found a place for us to live. An abandoned building not far from where we will set up business. There are other street kids living in the area, so no one will notice if a few more show up," he said with a slight smile.

"Tomorrow, when they open the gate, be ready to go out with the others. I will wait for you at the end of the block. Robert did not wait for an answer; he looked quickly both ways, put his hands in his front pockets and joined the street unnoticed.

At precisely one o'clock, one of the workers opened the front gates to the orphanage. There were thirty-six kids ready to go out to their apprenticeships. No one bothered to count or check the departing teens. The youngsters didn't run away very often; there was nowhere to run. Those who did leave were normally back within a few days. Two or three days with no food was enough time to convince them that the orphanage wasn't such a bad place after all.

When children did run away, the worker responsible for that group of kids would report the child missing. The supervisor would fill out a one-page form and take it to the orphanage superintendent. He would sign and stamp the form and have a courier take it to the central police station where it was filed. No one at the police station ever read it, and no one at the orphanage would do anything further. The important thing for them was the policy and procedure manual requirement had been met.

The only time the police would look through the missing orphans file was when a body of a child was found in the city with no identification. They would check to see if the general description on a report matched the body found. If it did, or was close to matching, the case was closed. No one wanted to spend much time or effort on street kids. They were nothing but trouble and one less on the streets was a good thing for the police.

The police clerk did not take a second look when the courier handed him an envelope. He opened it quickly to find a missing orphan form. He sat the form on the edge of his desk until he had time to file it in the back storage room. There, at the end of the center aisle, about waist high, was a large cardboard box. The clerk pulled it out just enough to be able to slip the form through a slot in the top. It fell into darkness.

Robert and Simon's new home was an empty room in an abandoned building. This was an area of the city that had many deserted buildings and many empty rooms. The room Robert chose had no windows; whatever glass had been there had been stolen long ago. No doors, no lights, nothing but concrete. Robert instructed Simon on the way to grab whatever newspapers or cardboard he could find; he did not say why. Twice they went into alleys and picked through heaps of garbage looking for the requested items; they were hard to find.

Robert was a fastidious dresser. He took great care not to get his clothes dirty. The cardboard was placed on the floor; it became both a chair and the bed. He explained that newspapers made good fuel for a fire. Wad them up tightly and they would burn like wood. That first night, Robert brewed some hot tea in a discarded tin can he found while looking for the paper and cardboard.

The fire was built in a bucket found under some garbage piled in the entryway. Their cup was the bottom portion of a blue plastic bottle that Robert had cut off with his knife. There was a common water spigot about two blocks away; no one in this part of the city had running water in their apartments. Robert sent Simon to fetch the water. While he was gone, Robert pulled a small bag of tea from his pocket. He had stolen it from a street vendor's cart.

The first night away from the orphanage was terrible for Simon. He missed his room. Even though it was crowded with five other boys, it was all he had ever known. Now he lay on a small piece of smelly cardboard in a dark room in an empty building. Simon felt afraid, so incredibly alone. The tears ran freely down the side of his face. They formed a pool of sadness on his hard bed. He was awakened several times during the night by strange noises; he looked closely to make sure Robert was still lying beside him. He was. It helped. But not nearly enough.

Chapter Twelve

Robert and Simon walked a few blocks together without speaking. They stopped and waited. Robert tapped Simon on the arm and started walking into the street; an ancient bus ambled around the corner. It did not stop but slowed down. People began stepping off, as others waited to jump on. There were no tickets, no doors, no windows, or seats. People clung just as easily to the outside as they did to the inner handholds.

Robert ran with the other riders to the back door and effortlessly jumped on the lower step. Simon did not know what to do, so he just ran beside the bus. Robert looked over his shoulder and saw Simon being left behind. He quickly reached back and grabbed Simon's arm and lifted him onto the narrow step next to him. Robert looked down at his young friend and smiled. He liked taking care of Simon; he felt like an older brother. They rode for fifteen minutes. Then reversed the mounting process. Simon had never ridden a public bus alone before and enjoyed the experience of moving so fast. He was smiling too.

It took a moment for Simon to notice that he was in another world. There were tall, bushy, green trees, beautifully manicured lawns and flower gardens, and expensive, modern shops. The large, stucco, white and light tan houses and marble covered buildings with darkened glass windows were beautiful. There were dozens of little black and white cars whizzing by, some stopping to pick up people, while others stopped to let others out. Simon had no idea what they were doing. "What are those little cars for?" Simon asked Robert, pointing to the little black and white vehicles darting in and out of traffic.

Robert let out a loud laugh "Simon, you don't know what a taxi is?" Robert slapped him on the back and walked across the street.

Colorful neon signs flashing in the store windows, people dressed in expensive western clothes, driving fancy imported cars; a policeman blowing his whistle and traffic stopping; it was all so wonderfully new and strange to Simon. The orphanage specialized in dull colors and drab, worn hand-me-downs.

They walked a few blocks from the river, down a manicured, tree-lined street. Robert looked Simon over very carefully. "He will be perfect for the job," he thought smugly.

Simon wore the only clothes he owned. His shirt was a light, faded yellow. It was supposed to be long sleeved, but the sleeve ended about four inches above his wrists. The elbows were worn thin and the second button from the top was missing. His pants had started out as white, but the constant wear and minimal washing made them look like light brown. There was a tear across the left knee. He wore black plastic sandals that were split across the top and two sizes too large.

"For now," Robert thought, "he is dressed just about right. But as business improves, we will have to get some nicer clothes." Robert liked Simon. His dark curly hair framed a gentle face. There was something about Simon that seemed so gentle. His large brown eyes made him appear almost animal-like, not a wild animal, more like a puppy. His skin was smooth and his lips were nicely formed and broke into an easy smile. No one ever felt threatened by Simon.

Not so with Robert. He was big and strong and agile. He reminded his friends of a large cat. He was quick to pounce on anything or any-one that he thought weaker than himself. He did not appear mean, just efficient. He had already killed two other boys. The drug dealer that had disappeared did so because Robert put a bullet through his head. It was nothing personal, just business. Robert felt no tinge of remorse. He did what he had to do to make his business plan operational.

Robert reached out and touched Simon on the arm. They were com-ing to the end of the block. Robert took the lead and slowed the pace. He cautiously approached the corner, looking intently one way and then the other. When satisfied they were safe, he motioned for Simon to come up next to him. "This is where we will set up business," Robert said proudly.

Simon looked up at his friend, his eyes questioning.

"Here's how it works. See that big wall across the street, the white one?" Simon leaned forward and looked in the direction where Robert pointed.

"That is the Cairo International School. All the foreign kids go there.

Their fathers are rich and so the kids have a lot of money to spend on drugs. There are three main dealers around here. There is one guy who sells at the other end of the block and one on the back-side of the school and us here. This is where the guy who disappeared used to sell. But now it is our territory." Robert looked away from Simon when he said this.

"Your job is to be the seller. You speak English pretty well so you should have no problem. Even if you didn't speak any English, you could do this with hand signals. Basically, they will tell you how many bags of hashish they want. Each bag is two dollars. They all know that, so it is very simple. Cash up front. Never give them the drugs without getting the money first. This is important Simon, do you understand?" Robert had his face close to Simon's. His eyes narrowed and his voice lowered.

Simon nodded.

"It doesn't matter if you have to kill other street kids or drug dealers. The police don't care. But if I have to hurt one of the foreign students," his voice trailed off, "well, it creates a lot of problems."

Simon's eyes got very wide. When Robert mentioned killing, his mouth went dry. "You never said anything about killing people," Simon said quietly.

Robert looked both ways up and down the street. "Simon, listen very carefully. This is not a game. This is life and death. There is no one to watch out for us; there is no one who cares what happens to us. If we are to survive, we must take care of ourselves. This business is deadly. You only get one mistake, but the potential is incredible. We can make more money in one month than most people make in a year. If we do it right, we can have whatever we want. Clothes, girls, an apartment — a real one, not some dump like now. But we have to establish ourselves. We must never show weakness." Robert's voice was steady.

"My job is the protector. You will be here on the corner. I will be across the street." He gave a slight nod with his head. "Everyone knows the drill. There is always one seller and one enforcer. If someone tries to cheat us, they get hurt real bad. They try and move in on our territory, they get dead." Robert reached down and pulled up the corner of his shirt tail slightly, just enough for Simon to see the handle of a gun.

Simon instinctively pulled back. He had never seen a real gun before. Just seeing it scared him.

Robert continued the lecture. "We arrive early enough each day to sell before school. We have to be back here around noon when they have a break for lunch and then here again after school. That's the best time to sell." Robert pulled a well-worn fanny pack around so it rested on his stomach. He unzipped it and began to count out small plastic bags of hashish.

Simon noticed a stack of bills next to the bags. They looked like American dollars and there must have been a hundred of them.

Robert saw Simon looking at the money. He smiled. "I told you this is a great business."

"If you have so much money, why don't you get a better place to live?" Simon asked.

"We are just starting out. This is our most vulnerable time so we must stay low profile. No one knows who we are or where we live; we will change buildings every three or four days. That way, no one can ambush us. Once we get established, get a reputation, then we can settle in and start some other businesses." Robert spoke like a seasoned veteran, not a seventeen-year-old street kid.

Simon was nervous the first morning he sold drugs. He was glad his English lessons in school paid off. He understood most of the words the kids said to him. At first he did not say anything back. He just gave them however many bags they wanted and made sure they gave him the correct amount of dollars.

During the day, instead of going back to the empty building, they would walk several blocks deeper into the wealthy neighborhood. There were some small shops along the way, they would buy some breakfast and smoke cigarettes and drink tea. Everyday they would meet a friend of Robert. He was an older man, with several teeth missing in the front of his oversized mouth. He wore a dirty, tattered, khaki-colored, canvas hat. His eyes were weasel-like; dark brown, constantly darting back and forth. He smelled like cigarette smoke and worked as a gardener at a very nice villa nearby. He was the man that Robert bought the bags of hashish from. The gardener bragged that he grew the hashish himself, right under the nose of the foreign renter. "White guys wouldn't know hashish from a petunia," he scoffed.

Over the next five months, business was very good. Robert and Simon made plenty of money and Robert found a small place to live. It was dirty and cheap, but at least it had a real bed and windows. It was home.

Simon liked his job. It did not take long before he developed a solid grasp of English. He could easily communicate with the buyers and his easy smile and warm disposition made him a favorite with the international school clientele. He was also honest — something they didn't usually find among drug dealers. He earned respect because he never tried to cheat them out of money or drugs.

Simon could tell Robert was getting restless. The days were full of activity, but the nights were empty. Robert and Simon would spend every night out with friends. They would drink and smoke hashish and party until the early morning hours. At first, Simon resisted. No one forced him to drink or do drugs, but the good feeling he felt from the stimulants helped him forget the emptiness. It was only a momentary relief; the loneliness and alienation came back, but at least it was a reprieve.

"We are wasting a lot of good time," Robert said one day as they were waiting for the students to get out of classes. "We could be making money at night as well." Robert looked at Simon. Simon took a slow drag on his cigarette, but said nothing. "Some of the girls we've been hanging out with could be very valuable. Did you notice the way some of the older men were looking at them?" Robert didn't wait for a reply. "If we started offering them for a good price, we could make money at night, as well as during the day." Robert had obviously been thinking of a new business plan.

"The principle is the same." Robert loved to teach. "Power is the key. The only way prostitution works is if the girls have someone to protect them. The client must know if he tries to cheat or abuse, I will be there to 'discourage' those kinds of behavior. So we provide the protection; well, I provide the protection. You are good at selling, so you will be the salesman. We just need to find some product." Robert chuckled at his own humor.

Simon and Robert started spending time near the orphanage. They knew several girls who would soon graduate. The orphan girls were the most vulnerable. After being processed out of the orphanage, they were on their own. They really didn't have a chance. Either unscrupulous merchants would be waiting to commit them to slave labor in their factories or agents for house workers would be waiting to sell them off to a life of hard labor working for rich families. Or there were guys like Robert, who would be waiting to offer protection, security, and a good time for the price of their bodies. For those who had a choice, Robert's proposition sounded the best. It wasn't.

The prostitution business was more complicated than the drug trade. Simon had to work hard to sell the product. He focused on the hotels where foreign businessmen stayed.

Simon now had a stylish wardrobe. He looked immaculate as he marketed young girls in the lobbies of the nicer hotels.

Robert sat with two or three girls across the street. When Simon made a sale, he would signal, and Robert would bring one of the girls over. The money was paid in advance and the girl would go upstairs with the client. Their business specialized in foreigners. For one thing, they paid more than the locals, and second, they didn't tend to abuse the merchandise as much.

Life was good. Robert and Simon were not necessarily happy, but they were successful. They had a prosperous drug trade by day and a solid prostitution business by night. One of the hidden problems of success, however, is that it is difficult to remain unnoticed. While Robert enjoyed his wealth and his power, there were those watching and waiting in the shadows.

After a particularly busy day in front of the school, Simon and Robert split up. Simon wanted a haircut and Robert returned to their apartment to change shirts. He had ripped his sleeve getting off the bus. He also needed to pick up the girls. They were to meet in front of the hotel at seven.

Simon arrived early and sat out of sight, waiting for Robert to arrive. By seven fifteen, Simon knew something was wrong. Robert was always a businessman first; he was never late. Simon jogged to where the girls stayed. They were all there waiting. Robert had not shown up.

Simon was now in a full panic. He ran as fast as he could to their flat. He stopped when he reached the landing for their floor. He looked closely. The door to their apartment was slightly ajar. He took a few steps and paused at the door, listening for any sound. There was none.

Slowly he pushed the door open; he crouched down and looked around the door. Much to his relief, everything was as they had left it. He continued to wait and listen. It was absolutely still. Simon stepped into the living room and looked toward the bedroom. The door was wide open, and he could see nothing unusual. He walked cautiously toward the door. Putting his hand on the doorframe, he peeked in.

Robert was lying on the bed. Hundreds of flies crawled over his lifeless face. Blood was splattered on the walls, the ceiling and the bed. A large pool of blood was under Robert's head, some smeared across his face. Simon remembered only the color red when he thought back on the scene. Robert's throat had been slit. Not a nice clean slit, but a massive gaping wound. It was like someone had wanted to cut Robert's head completely off. His eyes were fixed blankly on the ceiling. Robert was dead.

Simon vomited. It was a reflex response to a scene so horrific and terrifying that Simon did not even realize he had done it. The panic and fear were so powerful that he felt paralyzed. Everything within him wanted to turn and run, but he stood frozen.

Then, tears flooded his face; his breathing came in great, deep heaves. He wanted to move forward and comfort his friend, but instead he felt himself moving backwards. Stumbling and falling, he ran out the door and down the stairs to the street. He instinctively started to run toward the orphanage. Subconsciously, it was still home.

He feared someone would step out and slit his throat at any moment. He kept running. He found himself standing in a filthy room in an empty building, back where he and Robert had started. He thought of going to the police, but quickly realized that it would be foolish. They didn't care if another drug dealer had been killed. And they could easily assume he had killed Robert for the money or drugs and blame him. The case would be solved and he'd be in prison.

Simon shivered and shook with fear and sadness the entire night as he sat crouched in the filthy, empty room. He wept and groaned the loss of his friend. The only person he knew who cared for him, who really loved him, was dead. He was abandoned once again.

Simon spent nearly a week holed up in abandoned buildings. He went out at night, only to get food. He never went to the same place twice. He never went to a place where he might be recognized. He was sure that the guys who had killed Robert did so because of the prostitution. Whoever killed Robert had to have a more sophisticated operation than theirs. There had been some threats when they first started at the hotels; they thought the pimps were just trying to scare them off. No one cared much about the drug dealing at the school, or did they?

Simon disguised himself as best he could. He wore an oversized hat, pulled over his face. He walked around several additional blocks to get in the right position to see the school and his old territory. The streets were busy with students arriving for class. Sure enough, there was a young boy standing where Simon had stood. Simon looked across the street where a much older man watched the young boy sell. Robert and Simon had been bought out, drug style.

Simon leaned back against the small wall he was hiding behind. He closed his eyes. He had no idea what to do. He knew he could not go back to work without Robert to protect him. He needed to stay out of sight for a while. He removed the hat, the sun felt hot on his face. He liked this neighborhood; he felt comfortable here.

Simon cautiously made his way to the place he and Robert used to go when off duty. The gardener was sitting on his heels in front of his gate smoking a cigarette. He looked dejected.

Simon sat next to the man, not saying a word. The gardener ignored him. Without speaking, he held out the half-smoked cigarette to Simon who took it and inhaled deeply, blowing the smoke down at the ground.

"I heard about Robert." The man said. He looked straight ahead.

"How did you hear?" Simon asked.

"News travels fast. Seems he got too big, too greedy. People don't mind if you take little bites; but when you take too much too quickly ... well, that draws the attention of the big players. Robert knew it was a power thing. Trust me, Simon, there is always someone out there bigger and more powerful."

The man was now looking at Simon. "I am out of business too. You and Robert were my best customers. I am not going to sell on the streets; it's too risky."

"I'm not either. I need a place to hide for a while. Just to disappear." Simon took a final drag on the cigarette and stubbed it in the dirt beside him.

"There is a new guy here. He just moved in a several months ago." The gardener paused looking at Simon closely. He hesitated, obviously weighing something in his mind. The gardener was trying to decide if now was the time to proposition Simon. He was obviously scared and desperate, but the gardener decided to use the bait of safety very carefully. Twenty dollars a month was a great deal of money. He could not afford to waste the opportunity.

"You can stay here tonight. When the time is right I will talk to the master of the house and see if he will take you on as well." The gardener spoke in a soothing tone.

Simon sighed, relieved. He started to shake. He had barely eaten or slept for more than a week. The gardener led him to a small room near the swimming pool pump house. He brought him some food. Simon ate quickly and then fell into a deep sleep.

After a few days, when the time seemed right, the gardener approached Simon. "I think I might have a way for you to stay here and stay safe."

He lit a cigarette and handed it to Simon. "The man who is renting this house is an American. He is looking for a, well, a particular kind of young man. He has pretty specific requirements. You might fit his needs. He would offer you a place to stay on the premises, food, and a small salary. You would work with me in the garden. But you would be available, shall we say, for the master's pleasures at night." The gardener looked down at the ground.

Simon felt sick. He knew what the gardener was saying. He had been the pimp; he would never be the prostitute. Angrily, he started to get up.

The gardener put his hand on his arm. "Don't be in such a hurry. You would be safe here; I would take care of you."

Simon felt his skin tingle. He wanted to get up and run as far and as fast as he could. "You know the word on the street is that whoever killed Robert is still looking for you," he lied.

"I am not saying I would, but if I was to tell them where they could find you, they might want to start doing business with me again." The gardener removed his hand from Simon's arm. He waited a few seconds and said, "You're free to go ... if you want."

Simon stood and walked to the gate. He looked into the streets and halted. He was trapped. The gardener knew he could not strike out on his own. Simon hung his head in defeat fighting back the tears. The gardener rose slowly and walked over to where Simon stood. He took him by the arm and led him to his new home. Dr. Asbury would be very pleased.

Chapter Thirteen

Dr. Asbury took his new job very seriously. The first four months were spent visiting as many churches as possible. He initiated a church profile survey for each church in the country. To make good decisions, correct data was necessary. He did not say much, but asked a lot of questions and observed. A yellow legal-sized notepad, shipped from the States, was never far away; he wrote everything down.

Dr. Asbury finally turned his attention to his adopted home church. He liked the Reverend Habib, the senior pastor. The church was growing in numbers, was financially independent, and had several strong programs for the children, youth, and young professionals. The Reverend Habib appeared to be quite competent, a refreshing discovery. Dr. Asbury requested and received a list of all the services and ministries of the church. He began to visit them one by one.

On a Tuesday evening, he attended the young professionals meeting. He thought it might be interesting to see what caliber of people attended. He arrived late. The group consisted of about thirty people. A young man playing a guitar led the group. Thomas stood in the back looking for a place to observe from. They were finishing a song. Some had their hands raised, others were kneeling on the floor, and some were just sitting quietly. There was a peaceful silence.

Dr. Asbury found a seat at the back of the room. When the singing was finished, a young lady stood up and walked to the front. Dr. Asbury felt his stomach muscles tighten. She was actually quite beautiful; the young woman looked to be a few years younger than him. Before she said a word, Dr. Asbury decided he did not like her. She had an air of confidence and inner strength that threatened him. He thought she was going to make an announcement or introduce the speaker. But she did neither. Instead, she took out an old, worn Bible and a few pages of notes and began introducing the topic for the evening. Her English was exceptional; she was obviously a very intelligent and articulate woman. It was also obvious she was intending to teach the Bible study.

Dr. Asbury's knuckles went white as he tightened his grip on the arm of his chair. He wanted to jump up and shout this pretentious, power-hungry woman into submission. How could these people be so ignorant, after all the years of missionary activity, not to mention the millions of dollars poured into the churches here? Could they still be so incredibly stupid? He instantly hated the whole group; they were just as guilty by letting this abomination continue.

He stared at the woman leader with blazing contempt and anger, trying to will her to be silent; when that failed, he stood and stormed out of the room. A few heads turned to see who left, but most where too focused on what Rebekah was saying.

Dr. Asbury called an emergency meeting of the national council of elders. The council consisted of ten men, each representing a region of the country. They were the governing body for all the churches. Dr. Asbury dismissed the sitting chairman and demanded to chair the meeting himself.

There was no question of who was in charge. For more than an hour he went step by step over the observations he had made on his recent tours. With each point, Dr. Asbury became angrier. Under normal circumstances he was a strikingly handsome man. Even though his blonde hair had darkened as he grew older and he had gained some weight, his blue eyes were strong and clear and he maintained a certain youthful charm.

When angry, however, Dr. Asbury would undergo a physical transformation. At the beginning of the meeting, Thomas looked very much the part of a director of a mission agency. He was dressed in a very expensive navy blue suit and tie, white shirt, and polished shoes. He started out calmly, but as the diatribe continued his very countenance changed.

Spittle flew from the corners of his mouth; he was perspiring, stopping from time-to-time to wipe the beads of sweat from his face. His normally well-groomed hair was now wet and hanging over his forehead. His face contorted and twisted with every righteous word he spoke. His eyes actually changed color; they went from blue to an eerie yellow-green, bulging animal-like.

"This is a Bible-believing denomination. Do you understand that?"

He was shouting again. "We take the Scriptures seriously, literally. Paul meant what he said and said what he meant. When he said women should be silent in the churches, what do you think he meant?" He did not wait for an answer.

"When Paul said that a woman should not have authority over a man what did he mean?" Dr. Asbury was pacing back and forth, his arms flailing. The men in the room sat in silence, heads bowed, shoulders rounded in defeat. No one dared challenge or question the director.

"It is no wonder that you are not experiencing God's blessings, living in such sin and disobedience," he snarled. There was a long pause as he walked back to where he'd started. "I have only been here a few months and already have a list of more than a dozen church policy violations." He looked down at his list and began to read again to make sure they understood what he was talking about. "Clapping hands, swaying to the music in a sensual manner that entices lust, raising hands during the singing, some were heard to speak in tongues, going to dances, drinking alcohol, letting women lead and speak in church." His voice nearly cracked with fury by the end.

Dr. Asbury bent over the table and leaned close to the faces nearest him. "Gentlemen this must and WILL change," he spoke very slowly, enunciating each word. The yellow-green eyes slowly looking each one squarely in the face.

"We must begin putting our house in order. If we show true courage and do not back down, if we obey God's laws no matter what the cost, then we will have God's blessings." As the flame of fervor burned to an ember, Thomas slowly returned to normal.

"Reverend Habib, there is no better place to start than here." Mounir did not look up. Thomas continued in a calm tired voice. "If we make this church an example, the other churches will follow. We must set the standard. Some people may get their feelings hurt and some may leave, but we cannot abandon truth for the sake of a few people's feelings."

Thomas felt a sudden rush of emotional energy surge through his body. He loved to control and dominate situations and people. It gave him an almost euphoric feeling of invincibility. It didn't seem to matter if it was having sex with boys, overpowering his weak wife, or bringing a wayward church back to the straight and narrow way, the feeling was the same. He sat at the head of the table enjoying the intense emotion. The spell was broken when Reverend Habib spoke.

"What exactly do you propose, Dr. Asbury?" Pastor Habib asked.

Thomas raised his head slowly. He took a deep breath. "This young lady who leads the career and professionals meeting, what is her name?"

"Rebekah." Pastor Habib said softly.

"I am writing a five-year strategic plan for the denomination in this country. It includes a policy for church conformity; all of the churches under my authority will live up to the truth of Scripture. We need to make an example of this Rebekah woman; put the fear of God into the hearts of the people, so we can lead them properly." He paused and looked directly at Pastor Habib.

"Reverend Habib, I want you to call a meeting next week with the elders of your church. I want everyone there, including Rebekah. Don't tell her what it concerns. I do not want her trying to rally support and splitting the church. No, it needs to be a swift, clean chop." Thomas brought his raised hand down in a slicing motion.

Dr Asbury dismissed the meeting and walked to his car. The driver was leaning against the front fender on the passenger side. He moved forward and opened the door for Dr. Asbury.

Thomas was wet with perspiration, exhausted. For just a second, he had a flashback of T. Tucker. Now he knew how T. Tucker must have felt after the services. It was nearly ten o'clock before his car pulled up to the gate. The gardener opened the gate and allowed the car to pass. He then made sure it was tightly shut and locked.

When Thomas stepped out of the car, he saw the gardener walking toward him. "Good evening, Dr. Asbury," he said. Lowering his head slightly, he looked over his shoulder to see where the driver was. He asked, "Dr. Asbury may I have a word with you?" Thomas was still feeling the incredible high of the adrenaline rush from the meeting. He slung his jacket over his shoulder and walked next to the gardener as they strolled toward the swimming pool.

"I have found a fine young boy who needs a place to stay and needs work. I have checked him out, asked some friends; he is a very good boy. He grew up in an orphanage so there is no family. If he doesn't please you, at least it is a start; I might be able to find another. But it takes a lot of time and, well you know, discretion to find the right one."

Thomas smiled. He reached into his pocket and pulled out a large roll of dollars. He peeled off a twenty and handed it to the gardener.

"Give me half an hour and then send the boy to my bedroom. Have him use the garden entrance, not through the house." Thomas felt great power; he had absolute control. He could do anything he wanted and no one could challenge him. He liked being a missionary.

Chapter Fourteen

To Rebekah it seemed her entire life had been a constant fight to succeed, only to find herself pushed aside because of her gender.

She thought of her fight to get into medical school; there were only four women in her class. Trying to secure a position at the hospital took nearly two years, and then she was hired because no male doctors were available. When building her practice, people wanted to see a real doctor, not a woman. These were battles she was willing to endure. She knew she was as intellectually gifted and physically talented, but simply being a female was an insurmountable handicap. She had come to expect discrimination from her culture, but now to hit it head-on in the church was almost unbearable.

Her teacup sat half-emptied on the small table next to her chair. The chair was positioned so that she could look out through the glass doors, which led to a small balcony, and see the city. She loved the view from this window. Looking over the city gave her a sense of peace; just knowing she was not as alone as she felt was comforting. Normally her strength was solving difficult problems, breaking the problem down and solving it piece by piece. But she had to admit this was a dilemma not to be easily resolved. She just sat there rigid, pondering her inner turmoil.

"Who could I talk to? Who would understand? I do not want pity or patronizing answers or thoughtless responses; I need someone who can help me think through the issues and help me see the way — if there is a way. If not, then I will just have to accept the status quo and make the best of it." There was a deep sick feeling in the pit of her stomach.

"Oh, Lord, please help me! I feel so alone in this world, so small and utterly meaningless." The tears flowed freely, coursing down her smooth, olive skin. "I feel wounded inside, so many questions and so few answers. Lord please help me!"

Several weeks passed. Rebekah focused on her practice and calls at the hospital, burying her feelings under a heavy load of work. At her office, she was looking over her patient list and noticed that Elisabeth Aziz was scheduled for that afternoon. She knew Elisabeth from church; she was one of those ladies who exuded a natural sense of peace and graciousness. Her husband was a professor at the university and taught at the local seminary; but other than that she really did not know them well.

Rebekah was surprised as she walked into the consulting room to see both Elisabeth and Dr. Aziz sitting in the chairs waiting. After brief greetings, she got down to business. Elisabeth had not been feeling well for several months. Dr. Aziz was more worried than Elisabeth. He seemed a very caring and gentle man. Rebekah caught herself smiling. Dr. Aziz seemed to be the classic absent-minded professor.

He was a wiry little man, his oversized, brown, tweed jacket hung down over his shoulders. His hair looked as if it had gone weeks without brushing; he wore a rumpled pair of trousers and a shirt with cheap ball point pens hanging from the well-used pocket. His bushy eyebrows would have seemed menacing were it not for his warm, peaceful hazel eyes and gentle brow. Dr. Aziz paced the room while Rebekah asked Elisabeth questions and completed an initial examination.

After several visits and a long round of tests, the Aziz's became more than just patients; a friendship began to bloom. Rebekah felt relief when the tests came back. There was no life-threatening condition, and with regular medication, Elisabeth should be back to full-strength soon

She decided to stop by the Aziz's apartment on her way home to share the good news. "There is no reason to hurry back to my flat," she thought, "only an empty set of rooms waiting." Besides, over the weeks they had spent together, she grew fond of the gentle Elisabeth and the eccentric doctor.

On her way, she stopped at a local café for a drink and to collect her thoughts. Since meeting Dr. Aziz and Elisabeth, she had appreciated how kindly they treated each other. She wondered if she was attaching feelings that she might have had for her father, if she had known him, to Dr. Aziz. Elisabeth could have been everyone's mother, so sweet and caring.

They had raised four children, now grown and living abroad. She felt safe and accepted when she was with them. Perhaps Dr. Aziz would be someone she could talk with. He seemed very knowledgeable and, more importantly, understanding.

As Rebekah turned the corner and headed down the road to the Aziz's apartment, she started having second thoughts. She had better not ask Dr. Aziz anything. She would give them the welcomed report and leave. How could she ever find the inner strength to share so personally? Besides she was a professional and must keep a polite distance from her patients.

She rang the bell and Dr. Aziz opened the door. Immediately, his eyes showed fear to see Rebekah standing there. He expected the worst. Elisabeth came down the hall soon after and invited Rebekah into the parlor. As soon as they sat, Dr. Aziz anxiously asked, "Was the news bad?"

"No." Rebekah smiled. She then explained the results and told Elisabeth that with proper medication she should be fine. Everyone was so relieved, Dr Aziz walked over to where Elisabeth sat and gave her a kiss on the forehead and patted her shoulder. Elisabeth insisted on making tea and left the room. Rebekah considered protesting but in the end said nothing.

Rebekah sat silently with Dr. Aziz. He stood at the window, hands clasped behind his back. Without turning, he spoke to Rebekah. "You are carrying a very heavy burden, my dear. I can see the pain in your eyes and feel your despair." Rebekah was shocked; she thought she did a good job of covering up her emotions.

Dr. Aziz turned from the window and walked over to where Rebekah was sitting. He sat down beside her. "I certainly do not want to intrude on your private life, but Elisabeth and I would think it an honor to talk with you and help however we can. We so appreciate the way you have cared for Elisabeth; you have been so very kind."

His gentle and caring voice dissolved her fears. She began haltingly, first telling of her confusion and her hurt from Dr. Asbury and the elders board, her questions about a woman's role and the Scriptures, the feelings of rejection and the sadness in her spirit. She'd barely begun speaking when Elisabeth returned with the tea. She placed it on the table and sat quietly on the other side of Rebekah, gently resting her hand on her new friend's arm.

Through her tears, Rebekah continued. It was like someone peeling an onion; layer-by-layer, she went deeper. Rebekah had never told anyone, not even Miss Lovejoy, of the rape and pregnancy and the abandonment of her son. But it all poured out, uncontrolled, like a raging tide.

It was as if she could not stop the flood. Finally, no more words would come only salty tears.

Rebekah crumpled beneath the weight of condemnation and guilt and buried her head in Elisabeth's lap. She felt so ashamed, so deeply shamed. Elisabeth's gentle hands stroked her back and it made Rebekah feel warm inside; the warmth of a mother's touch was more healing than any medicine. Rebekah didn't know how long she had laid there crying, but eventually the tears stopped, the heaving sobs subsided, she sat up, and sighing deeply, regained her composure. Elisabeth left to get some tissues. "I must look a mess," Rebekah thought, "and now that they know who I really am, this will end our friendship." She felt vulnerable.

Chapter Fifteen

Rebekah immediately regretted unburdening herself. But as she looked up and saw the look on Dr. Aziz's face, she saw his profound anguish. Sad, moist eyes, the corners of his wrinkled mouth turned down, his bushy eyebrows drooping. Elisabeth returned and handed Rebekah a tissue. Elisabeth again sat close beside Rebekah, head bowed, with silent tears running down her own face.

No one spoke or moved for a very long time. It was not an awkward silence. No one seemed in a hurry to say or do anything. There was, in a strange way, a peace blanketing the room. Dr. Aziz turned his head slightly and looked at Rebekah; he felt a deep pain as though someone had stabbed him with a very dull knife. A knot of grief made swallowing hard.

"So young, so talented," he thought. "Such a heart to serve and no way for her to obey His command to follow and to use her talents." Dr. Aziz had two deep feelings surging within both fighting to be the first one out: anger and shame.

The anger was easily identified. He had experienced it many times when he had encountered injustice, both in Egypt, because he was a Christian in a Moslem country, and during his studies abroad, because he was a foreigner. Discrimination was certainly no stranger to him. His brown skin and Arab features were enough; he was in the minority. And strictly because of his race, he had been treated with disdain. Every time it hurt and each time he felt the anger grow. He identified more deeply with Rebekah than she would ever know.

The second feeling had also been his familiar companion. He had felt it as a boy when he had disappointed his father or in school when he had done poorly on an exam. When he went to England to study, he felt it acutely the first days in class; his shabby clothes, outdated manners, and accented speech identified him as a foreigner.

The shame. No matter how hard he tried to be the best, the

smartest, the most accomplished, he could not live down the sense of having somehow failed. He thought the academic degrees that now hung on his office wall or the letters after his name would make it all better. But through these many years he learned to silently carry his own racial shame. And now it was back again. Only now he was shamed to be a man and a Christian.

There was no doubt in Dr. Aziz's mind why he felt the shame so acutely just now. He always had an insatiable curiosity. He could never just accept something that he was told; he always had to know why. This caused him a lot of trouble in school, where rote responses were preferred. At university he had no clue what he wanted to do; he just loved learning. He entered a course in philosophy and there he found his passion. Instead of being punished for asking too many questions, he was now expected to question everything. It was so much fun. It was also at university that he had met Christ. From the very beginning there was tension.

How could he pursue his love of philosophy and be a good Christian? One required him to question and the other required him to just believe. It was an agonizing time. He dared not tell his Christian friends of his struggle; he could not seem to find anyone in whom he could honestly confide. If they knew of his struggles, they would surely say his faith was weak. It was a relief when he arrived in London to study for his doctorate.

Much to his surprise, in his very first year at Oxford, he was assigned to a mentor who was both a philosophy professor and a Christian. This man had been such a wonderful friend and teacher. Dr. McCoy encouraged him to obtain dual degrees in philosophy and New Testament studies. He followed this advice and it changed his life. He promised himself and Dr. McCoy that if he ever got the chance he would give the same mentoring to others.

When he returned home to Cairo, he was offered a position as a professor of philosophy at the state university. In addition, he taught part time at the local seminary. He wanted so badly to be successful that he worked non-stop writing papers, giving lectures, traveling abroad, and building a reputation. He promised Elisabeth when they first met that he would not work so much once he established a reputation.

Unfortunately, once the appetite for recognition had been created, it was not easily satisfied. He could not resist the temptation when speaking invitations arrived, so he broke the promise to his precious Elisabeth and traveled on. Even when the children were born, he was often gone; he was there for two of the four births, two girls and two boys.

It surprised him how completely he had fallen in love with his girls. Of course, there would always be strong bonds with his sons, but it was his daughters that so captured his heart. It was a love he never knew was inside him, different from his love for Elisabeth but just as real and strong.

It seemed now like a blur, from childhood to young adults. One day they were walking down the street clinging to his hand and the next thing he knew, he was kissing them goodbye. One by one, they headed off to university. His sons had done very well in school; he was very proud. With some of his connections, they had been accepted to well-regarded universities and both were now living and working in Canada.

But Dr. Aziz was quick to notice that his girls were just as bright intellectually and worked harder than his sons, but they were always placed below the boys in the class standings. He knew early on that the only way for them to fulfill their potential was to move abroad. He had never shared that with anyone, not even Elisabeth. For it shamed him that he knew so well the injustice and he said or did nothing to oppose it. Even in church, the women were treated with contempt; somehow they were considered lower creatures than the men. It was no different in the pagan culture in which they lived. And yet he said nothing.

Rebekah's heart-wrenching words had triggered all these memories and more. He sat motionless unable to speak. The moistness around his eyes slowly turned to droplets of tears that coursed down his cheeks, following the pathway of his well-defined wrinkles. He dropped his sorrowful face into his hands and wept softly. Not only for Rebekah, but for his daughters living so far away and for the girls in his country who would know the pain of discrimination and abuse with no one to speak on their behalf. Who would help them?

One of Dr. Aziz's strengths was his ability to lose himself in thought. He would sometimes sit and ponder for hours losing track of time, appointments, teaching schedules; it was part of his legendary eccentricity. When he finally raised his head, he realized the room was now dark. Rebekah was gone. He heard Elisabeth washing the dishes in the kitchen. He immediately felt devastated that he had not said something to Rebekah or walked her to the door.

Chapter Sixteen

It was the secretary who first noticed the change in Dr. Aziz's schedule. She worked for six of the professors. He began arriving earlier and staying later. When she went into his office, a place notorious for looking like a cyclone disaster area, it had been rearranged and the books and papers stacked in a somewhat orderly manner. Scattered on the desk, the floor, and any available flat surface were papers neatly arranged, books opened and marked, with several pads of writing paper by each stack. Dr. Aziz was obviously on a mission. She had been with him for more than twenty years and she knew all the signs of research-in-progress.

It had been many months since Rebekah had last seen the Dr. and Mrs. Aziz. She was embarrassed to have imposed on them the way she had. It violated doctor/patient ethics, social and cultural mores; they weren't family or even close friends. She stopped going to church, too embarrassed to see them again.

Her refuge was her work. It kept her mind occupied, and with a busy schedule, she had little time to feel the pain. Work was like a drug. One morning, her receptionist handed her a note as she passed by the front desk. She had forgotten about it until later in the day when she reached in her pocket and found the crumpled piece of paper. It was from Dr. Aziz. He wanted to know if she could come for dinner next week. Her first thought was to make an excuse and not go.

Elisabeth answered the door. She offered Rebekah a warm embrace, kissed her gently on the cheek, and welcomed her. They went into the sitting room; Rebekah loved the smell in this room. It smelled like home or at least what she thought a home should smell like. They talked for a few minutes when Dr. Aziz appeared in the door. He saw Rebekah and a warm smile spread quickly across his face. He walked to where she sat and took her hand in both of his.

"How lovely to see you, Rebekah," he said; his words and eyes exuding sincerity and warmth. "Thank you for coming." He patted her hand as he spoke, not in a patronizing way, but in a manner showing genuine affection. His eyes sparkled and his eyebrows moved up and down as he spoke.

After dinner, Dr. Aziz asked Rebekah to join him in the study. Elisabeth entered a few minutes later with steaming tea and sweets. Rebekah saw the stacks of writing pads lined upon his desk and books arranged methodically on the floor. His office had changed since her last visit, not as messy but still not neat.

"Rebekah, my child, I am so profoundly sorry for the things you have gone through." His voice was low and comforting. No man had ever said those words to her before. It took away some of her uneasiness. When he said "my child" she smiled slightly. She was almost thirty years old, but the sound of those words soothed her soul like a warm hand placed on a child's heart. She had never heard them spoken with such love and tenderness. "Since our last visit I have spent a great deal of time pondering, thinking, and doing some research. You, of course, had no way of knowing my personal struggles intellectually and doctrinally with the issues you raised."

He went on quickly, "When I was at university working on my doctorate, I had a professor, Dr. McCoy, who took me under his wing and mentored me through the most challenging time of my life. I can honestly say that without his help, and of course the Lord's, I would never have made it through my studies."

His voice became husky and emotional. "I promised myself that I would someday do the same thing for my students, but I never did. Oh sure, I would meet with some who pursued me, but mostly I met with only the very brightest and best. It would look better on my record to have the best students saying that Dr. Aziz spent time with them. Rebekah, I can honestly say I was supremely selfish, only thinking of my own reputation. After our last visit I have spent considerable time repenting, asking God to forgive and cleanse me for my sin. For that is what it was Rebekah, pure and simple, sin."

Rebekah glanced at Elisabeth; she was seated just to her left and was looking up at Dr. Aziz, her face full of pride and pleasure. Dr. Aziz must have processed everything these many months with Elisabeth: his struggles, his failures, his sin. He began his famous pacing. Dr. Aziz walked back and forth when he lectured or spoke at seminars, and began doing it now.

"Besides repenting for the past wrongs, I have also given a good deal of thought to the future. I estimate I have no more than ten productive years left, the Lord willing. Rebekah, I want these remaining years to count. I can no longer remain silent when I see injustice, in or outside of the church. I must speak out."

Walking to his desk he took the top writing pad and began to pensively review his notes. "Rebekah if you are willing to be a diligent student, I would be proud to work with you in discovering some very wonderful truths about God and Scripture. I want to make good on my promise to my mentor, Dr. McCoy. It will be a wonderful journey of self-discovery."

"I will not simply give you the answers; a good teacher never does. But I will guide you and ask questions and give you the information you need to find the truth. Of course it is the Holy Spirit who empowers us to discover God's truth, but we must also be good stewards and use faithfully the gifts God has given us. I am referring of course to our minds and intellects. So this will not be easy, but nothing of value ever is." Dr. Aziz was now looking at her very intensely, his eyes almost ablaze with excitement and enthusiasm. "Rebekah, are you interested in starting this journey of discovery, a journey that in some ways will never end?"

Rebekah was caught off guard. She had no idea he would make such a proposal. Yet she immediately felt a sense of excitement, but also fear.

"What if I can't keep up with this great scholar," she thought. "I am certainly no philosopher or theologian and I hate sitting for hours on end listening to someone lecture. Maybe this isn't such a good idea."

It was as though Dr. Aziz was reading her thoughts. "Rebekah, this is not going to be some kind of class like you had at university, where the boring professor would lecture for hours and you would take notes and then regurgitate information. No, this will be done in the very best way to truly teach values. I will not just offer information; it will require self-discovery. This is how Jesus taught his disciples and his followers and there was no finer teacher than the Lord."

"How does it work?" Rebekah responded.

"Well, let's start by laying down some ground rules. First and foremost, questions are good. There are no silly or stupid questions; every question you ask will be taken seriously."

"Second, I know you are wanting to find answers for your very deep and personal situation and this is okay. However, it is imperative that when you read Scriptures you do not primarily look for answers. The questions asked of the text must not be 'What is the answer?' but 'What does the text say?'

"And finally, we must be willing to submit to the truth of the text regardless of our personal emotions and thoughts."

"But, Dr. Aziz, that's like putting your brain on the shelf and blindly saying you will obey before you know?" As soon as she realized what she had said, she felt embarrassed. A younger person was not to speak so openly to an elder, especially one as distinguished as this. But rather than being offended, she saw a wry smile unfold across his face.

"That is precisely the type of question I expect from a good student. The truth of Scripture is objective. It is outside of us. Therefore parts of it stand transcendent, truth for all time. But to know God's truth requires a certain honesty on our part. We must be willing to do it before we know it. Otherwise we put ourselves above the truth and decide what we will and will not do. This destroys the nature and power of the truth to change us. I might add that this is at the very heart of many of the problems facing our church today.

"Rebekah, I know it is getting late. I do not want to keep you. Tonight was not really meant to start our journey as much as it was to find out if you want to make the journey. You do not need to give me your answer now. Give it some serious thought and prayer and let me know."

During the next two weeks, between hospital calls and seeing patients, Rebekah pondered Dr. Aziz's proposition. Part of her was excited and wanted to begin the journey immediately. Another part hesitated, caught in a dilemma. What if Scriptures did declare women have no role in the church? Are they to be silent, submissive and subjugated to men. What then?

She honestly didn't know. Again her mind was of two thoughts. The priority was to just love Jesus; keep that relationship healthy. But how could she live with such hypocrisy, bigotry, and injustice within the church? Rebekah felt trapped; she could not go back and was fearful to move forward.

To be polite Rebekah decided to go to her first session with Dr. Aziz.

As she walked into Dr. Aziz's study, he was already pacing as if warming up for a race. She sat quietly in what by now had become "her seat" and placed her bag on the floor and tried to look attentive; Dr. Aziz did not speak for what seemed like a long time. When he did, his voice was soft and soothing and gentle.

"I can see, Rebekah, that you are not ready for the journey to begin." His words startled her; not in a frightening way, but in the way you are surprised when another knows your thoughts. Was she really that easy to read or was he an expert reader? She suspected it was a bit of both.

To try and hide her feelings from Dr. Aziz would be futile; she might as well be honest. She explained her concern of losing her personal relationship with the Lord if she pursued the academic route. Finding answers that might make her life more bearable could also undermine the simple love she now had for Christ.

Although she wasn't willing to do anything that might jeopardize her walk with Christ, she honestly did not know if she could continue or even want to associate with a church that was so narrow and bigoted. When finished, she looked up at Dr. Aziz, not knowing what to expect.

Rather than a stern look of disapproval on her mentor's face, she thought she saw a very satisfied glance as he walked by on his way to the window. He stood looking over the city, his back to her, for several minutes. Finally, he spoke.

"I have found over these many years that those who move rapidly and hurry to get on the road are most often the ones who never finish. Those who do not ask and face their primary fears ahead of time, later find an excuse to terminate their journey. No, Rebekah my dear, your fears are to be taken seriously, but examined in the light of Christ himself."

"But does it reflect a lack of faith on my part that I am afraid to trust the Lord and feel fearful to go into the unknown?" Her voice revealed a tinge of genuine anguish.

"Actually, it is quite a common fear among Christians," he said. "They think academic learning and loving Jesus are mutually exclusive. When you take this thinking to its reasonable conclusion, should one seek to be more ignorant so one can love Jesus more? I think not. We sometimes forget that it was Christ who said we would know the truth and it would set us free. It is the truth about Him that is our freedom.

But truth is a powerful thing and simply knowing it is very different from doing it." He started his rhythmic pacing again.

"Is it possible to start the journey slowly and take it a step at a time?" Rebekah asked.

"That's the only way to do it responsibly," Dr. Aziz said, halting his steps to looking out the window again.

He turned and walked to his desk where he picked up one of the many writing pads. He studied it briefly and simply said, "Let's begin."

"Rebekah, I need to make some introductory remarks," he said. "Most Christians should and hopefully do read their Bibles regularly as devotional material. Sometimes verses or ideas will jump from the page and we are arrested by their particular application. Perhaps we are sad and we read Paul's admonition to 'rejoice in the Lord always' and we feel encouraged. This approach is good for personal instruction and personal growth.

"However, it introduces some problems. If I read a passage that means something in particular to me and you read the same passage and it says something entirely different to you, who is correct?"

There was a long pause; it suddenly dawned on Rebekah that Dr. Aziz was waiting for her to answer. "I am not sure who would be right," Rebekah said quietly.

"In a sense, as long as we keep it to ourselves, it doesn't matter," he continued. "But when we start sharing it around as personal revelation, saying 'this is what this verse means for everyone,' it can then become problematic.

"This is how many of the cults and sects get their start, so we must have some guide, some standard by which Scripture is interpreted that is objective. Fortunately there is such a general guide and we will get to it shortly.

"I know from personal experience in the seminary that those of you who come from a science background tend to struggle a bit more. This is because you are used to having clear answers that everyone agrees upon. For example, Rebekah two plus two equals four. You would agree with this I presume?" Rebekah nodded her agreement.

"I assume your colleagues in Europe would agree, not so?" Again a nod of agreement. "The world of Bible translation and interpretation is not always so nicely packaged as the tenants of math and science. Many times the best answer is: 'I do not know' or 'Here are three plausible possibilities,' and 'we must choose the one that makes best sense of the text.' Can you imagine a math professor saying two plus two equals, and then giving a student three choices — each one of which may be correct?"

"But, Dr. Aziz, this is exactly what I was afraid of. Once we start asking questions and opening the door, where does it stop? Suddenly all the things that I thought were true may not be true at all, or at least not what I believed them to be. The ramifications scare me. Doesn't the Bible simply say what it means and mean what it says?"

Elisabeth walked into the room carrying a tray of tea and some sweet snacks. She poured the tea for everyone and then sat next to Rebekah. Rebekah felt the warmth of Elisabeth's presence; it comforted her. She had started to feel a fearful inner chill.

"You beat me to my next point. Oh, and thank you Elisabeth for your kindness; tea always has a way of invigorating one's soul." He smiled. He turned and carrying his tea in one hand, gestured with his free hand at the hundreds of books lining his library wall.

"Of all the books ever written regarding Scripture and all that will ever be written, there are common fundamental truths. All who call themselves believing Christians, and notice I must qualify this statement with the word 'believing' will acknowledge these shared truths: the deity of Christ, the death and resurrection of Christ, the fall of man, his need for redemption, salvation by faith ... and we could go on. But the point is, the Bible makes the core values of faith very clear. These are stated repeatedly with no contradictions to the essential truths. And while there may be some variations of emphasis on these fundamental issues, they are concepts upon which believers agree."

"Why is it so hard then to come to common understanding of all Scripture?" Rebekah interrupted.

Dr Aziz looked at his watch, "An excellent question, my dear, but it must wait for another time. I think we have opened enough doors for one evening. Be patient, Rebekah, we are laying the foundation for our future discussions; it may be a bit boring, but its necessary," Dr. Aziz said as he walked Rebekah to the door.

Chapter Seventeen

By now, Rebekah knew her way to the Aziz flat as well as to her own. It had become a wonderful routine: Dr. Aziz at the door and Elisabeth fixing tea. She felt at home. There was never a formal beginning. Dr. Aziz would simply start talking.

"The last time you were here Rebekah, you concluded with a very important question. Why are we not as clear on all the Scripture as we are on what we called the core values of the New Testament? The problem, at least for us, lies in the nature of Scripture and how it arrived into the twenty-first century.

"Each of the books comprising the New Testament were conditioned by the culture of the day: the language, the social mores, the political influences, the philosophies, and other religions. As you know the documents were written nearly two thousand years ago." He stopped and looked directly at Rebekah and paused.

"Tell me, Rebekah, what DO you know about how the New Testament was written?"

There was a brief silence as Rebekah looked first at her mentor and then at his impressive library. She thought, "Dr. Aziz probably knows all the information in all those books and I am supposed to give him an intelligent answer?"

"I know that the gospels were written by the disciples, although I don't think Mark was actually a disciple. The apostle Paul wrote a lot of the books and John wrote some and so did Peter. That's about it. Oh, Luke wrote Acts," she guessed. "To be honest I do not know very much about how the New Testament was put together," she thought to herself.

"I see we need a bit of a review," Dr. Aziz said. It was not a rebuke. "The New Testament, as we know it today, consists of twenty-seven books. They are divided into the four Gospels, one book of church history, twenty-one letters, and one Apocalypse. It was not until 367 AD that the first list of the New Testament documents we use today was defined." Dr. Aziz drew his handkerchief out of his back pocket and blew his nose.

"A wonderful Egyptian bishop, one of our own, Athanasius of Alexandria, sent an Easter greeting to his churches in the Spring of 367; he included a list of writings of those documents to be accepted by the churches of his diocese. Of course, there had been and were hundreds if not thousands of documents being passed among the various churches where Christianity had spread. The different churches each had their own collection of letters they deemed valuable. But no two churches had the same set. For example, the churches in Gaul, present day France, may have never heard of the letters used by the churches in Abyssnia; we know it as Ethiopia today. So it took nearly three hundred years to settle on a generally accepted set of documents." Rebekah shifted on the couch trying to find a comfortable position.

"This was not the first attempt. In 140 AD, a wealthy shipping merchant came to Rome from a town on the Black Sea. His name was Marcion. About 150 AD, he compiled a list of books he thought most valuable. However there was a small problem with Marcion, he was a heretic. Many of his ideas and teachings were not Christian at all."

Dr. Aziz started his evening walk. "So, although he could have done great harm to the church, he did gather the earliest known list of documents he thought to be genuine. His compilation included Paul's letters and Luke's Gospel, although Marcion rewrote parts with his own ideas."

Rebekah reached for her bag to get a pen and notepad, but her mentor did not slow his pace. "Marcion's attempt to manipulate the writings to prove his heresy jolted the church leaders to define a list of writings they thought to be genuine and important for the church to preserve.

"Shortly thereafter, in 170 AD, there appeared another list, most likely in response to Marcion's. It was called the Muratorian Canon. This list included the four Gospels: Acts, Paul's letters, Jude, First and Second John, and Revelation. It also had the book of the Wisdom of Solomon and possibly a second Apocalypse, one from Peter. Of more interest, perhaps, is what was left out: First Peter, James, Second Peter, Third John, and Hebrews. The attempt to identify the documents considered most valid continued up till the time of Athanasius."

"But that raises a lot of questions," Rebekah blurted out.

"Why did it take almost four hundred years before they finally had a complete set? You also said there were hundreds, if not thousands, of other documents, how did they decide which ones made it in and which ones were left out? Also how did they decide when the list was complete and not let anymore in and..."

"Please, Rebekah, I can only take one question at a time," Dr Aziz protested. "Let me see if I can give you an overview that may answer some of your questions. Toward the end of the second century, another heretic appeared that caused the church to think through what they accepted. A man named Montanus began teaching in a region called Phrygia, modern-day Turkey. He declared that the church was becoming too worldly, needed stricter guidelines, and that the second coming of Jesus was very close at hand.

"He also claimed that God had given him a special gift and that when he spoke under the guidance of the Holy Spirit, he was actually speaking for God. By inference, he claimed to be the promised 'paraclete' that Jesus had spoken of. You remember, the 'comforter' in John's gospel.

"Anyway, Montanus made a strong appeal to return to a more orthodox faith, but it was an orthodoxy of his own design. He was very articulate and intelligent; he deceived many and had a large following throughout the church. Even the great early churchman, Tertullian, was swept up into the heresy." Dr. Aziz seemed to take this heresy personally; he frowned when he spoke of Montanus.

"This profoundly worried the church leaders. To protect the people from further false teaching, they declared that all the sacred books that were to be written had been written so that Scripture as we know it today was closed." Dr. Aziz paused to collect his thoughts.

"They had shut the door to future writings, but they were not certain what to do with what they had. At that point there certainly was no agreement as to which of the many surviving documents were valid and which were not." His voice trailed off.

Dr. Aziz paused and looked at the door; he was ready for his tea. "Generally, there were three types of documents. Those that were accepted without reservation; most likely these were well known by a wide body of churches and the authorship uncontested.

"Then there were the documents somewhere in the middle. They did not really shed any new light on what Jesus said and were not found to be helpful to the churches in general.

"And finally, there were those works that were suspicious from the beginning. Normally these writings did not have a good reputation outside of a geographic region.

"It was a general rule, to be authentic the document must have had some direct apostolic connection. For example Ireneaus, one of the earliest writers, tells us that Mark was the interpreter for and a disciple of the Apostle Peter. Luke, a Gentile, worked closely with Paul. So their writings were readily accepted.

"One other thing before we move on — this will help us later. The letters of Paul are most certainly the first of the documents written. The oldest letter, the one to the Galatians, dates close to 49 AD and the latest one at around 62 AD. By 70 AD or so, most of the original apostles were dead. Seeing the demise of people who saw and heard firsthand what Jesus said and did, their friends and disciples began to gather authentic written accounts."

"How do you know all this information?" Rebekah said as she reached over to help Elisabeth set down the tray of tea.

Rebekah looked forward to the time when Elisabeth would join them. The routine seemed set. Rebekah would arrive, Dr. Aziz would greet her, they would talk for about thirty minutes in his office, then Elisabeth would appear with a drink and a snack. Elisabeth would join them for the duration, sitting next to Rebekah on a small, well-worn couch. Rebekah was not sure what she enjoyed more; the teaching of Dr. Aziz or the warmth of Elisabeth's presence.

Many times, just sitting next to Elisabeth and hearing the soothing voice of Dr. Aziz elicited the most secure feeling she had ever known. Rebekah would literally try to soak it in. She sometimes wondered if this was what it would be like to be in a loving family.

"Well, my dear Rebekah, this is a lifetime of learning. I was never the smartest kid in my class; my teachers would never have expected me to do well. And to be honest, I was somewhat lazy. But one thing I have always had was a deep sense of curiosity. I always wanted to know what made things work, why people did what they did, why they thought the things they thought, and so on. As I mentioned before, university was so refreshing; instead of being punished for asking, I was now encouraged to think for myself. The learning was secondary. It was a way to answer my own questions." He looked at the teapot, indicating he was ready for his cup of tea. Elisabeth ignored him. She was the master of the pot and only at her discretion would the tea be ready to be poured.

Dr. Aziz looked hurt, but he continued. "I did however, find it very curious. It was much easier to question ... really ask the hard questions ... in my philosophy classes than in the Biblical studies classes. My colleagues at the university here ask much better questions than my fellow professors at the seminary. As Christians, it seems as though there is a fundamental fear to question. So the result is many generations of folks who have not thought through what they believe and why they believe it; they just accept what has been told to them.

"I believe this makes for a very shallow faith. It concerns me when I see the students at the seminary, who will soon be the pastors of this nation, go out the door without exploring the most important questions of life. We seem to be satisfied placing empty hands on empty heads and sending them forth," Dr. Aziz said with conviction.

"Ishmael," Elisabeth said, "that was not kind."

Rebekah sat quietly, feeling uncomfortable. She had never heard Dr. Aziz's first name before. She never had ever thought of calling him anything but Dr. Aziz, but she thought it wonderful to know his given name. It seemed like an invisible barrier had been lifted. She was a step closer to knowing Dr. Aziz better. Also, she had never heard Elisabeth correct or challenge her husband. She started to get afraid. How would Dr. Aziz react? She hated confrontation. She could feel the tension within her build.

Dr. Aziz seemed to not hear his wife; he simply walked back toward his empty teacup, perched on the window ledge, waiting for Elisabeth's decree. "I know that was not charitable; I am sorry my dear, but I do get frustrated."

Chapter Eighteen

The days between the sessions flew by. Rebekah looked forward to the evenings spent with the Azizes. She had originally assumed Dr. Aziz would simply give her a few Scriptures to read pertaining to her questions and that would be the end of it. But when he started talking about finding truth as a journey, a process, a discovery, the effort took on new meaning.

The next time they met, Rebekah took her place on the sofa, took her purse from her shoulder, and laid it close to her feet. Rather than looking up at Dr. Aziz who had already begun to shuffle papers on his desk, she looked out the window. Dr. Aziz had started speaking, but Rebekah was preoccupied. Suddenly the room was silent.

"Rebekah, is everything all right?" he asked. He walked around to the front of his desk and stood by her.

"I am so discouraged," she said. "This past week, I was thinking about what you have shared. It was something entirely new and I found it enlightening. I was chatting with one of the nurses on Wednesday and was telling her of what you had said. A doctor friend overheard our conversation and joined in — uninvited I might add." She looked upset.

"He ridiculed us. Said the Bible was nothing but a bunch of fairy-tales and myths. That science had proven the New Testament was historically unreliable and contradicted itself and therefore could not be believed. He lived in the United States for many years and said even in a Christian nation very few people believe the Bible is for today's world." She looked up expecting Dr. Aziz to be irritated.

He stood for a long moment with his hands clasped behind his back. He turned on his heel and said, "Excellent, my dear, this is perfect."

"Excellent?" Rebekah squealed in protest. "I am all upset and discouraged and you think this is excellent?" She tried to sound angry but didn't.

Her mentor smiled. He enjoyed his time with Rebekah; they had an easy understanding of one another.

"Truth is not learned in a vacuum, Rebekah. What we learn must be tempered with real world experiences. This helps keep us balanced and relevant. If you get upset and defensive when people attack or don't appreciate our beliefs, then you will be upset a great portion of your life.

"Besides, this fits well with the next topic. In a sense, your doctor friend was doing what a lot of Christians do: repeating information he has heard or read without investigating the truth for himself."

For a moment, Rebekah thought he was speaking specifically of her, but quickly realized he was speaking of the church in general. "The reliability of the New Testament has long been a question of debate; not just in our time but since the very first century. One of the problems facing us today is the historical distance of nearly two thousand years, plus the fact that none of the original documents exist."

"What?" Rebekah exclaimed. "'You mean to tell me there are no original documents?" Rebekah felt uncomfortable now and wished Elisabeth would hurry up and come into the room.

"From a historical perspective, this is not as much of a problem as it may seem. The ancient world was not a literary world, for the most part. Of course there were no printing presses so every document that was produced was copied by hand. There was a whole profession dedicated to providing a copying service.

"Unfortunately, most of what became Scripture was copied by amateurs, causing a good deal of corruption to the originals. None of the originals exist from any of the great writers of antiquity. But most historians accept the copies as genuine expressions of the author.

"For example, no good historian doubts that Herodotus, the wonderful Greek historian who lived and wrote between 488 – 428 BC, authored the documents we know today. Yet there are only eight copies. The earliest in existence that we know of is from around 900 AD. That is a gap of more than thirteen hundred years.

"Another example is the Roman historian, Livy. He wrote a very good account of the history of Rome called Roman History. Again no good scholar doubts the authenticity of Livy, but the earliest manuscript copies go back to 900 AD. There are only twenty copies, and yet when written, Jesus could have very well been alive. So here is a gap of nearly 900 years." Dr. Aziz was speaking with his steady smooth voice.

"Now, when we come to the New Testament documents, from a purely historical perspective, we have overwhelming evidence of their authenticity and veracity. Just listen to this." Rebekah could tell when Dr. Aziz was getting excited. His voice would rise, his pacing sped up, and his arms would flail. It was not unusual for him to knock a book off the desk, hit the lampshade, or drop papers from his hand in his uncoordinated excitement.

"We have more than five thousand copies of Greek texts, more than ten thousand Latin copies, and nine thousand three hundred other documents written in other ancient languages. Plus nearly thirty-six thousand ... Rebekah, are you listening?"

He moved closer to where she was sitting. "I repeat, thirty-six thousand citings of these documents from the early church-fathers' writings. Your doctor friend may be a fine physician but would prove a poor historian," Dr. Aziz said with just a hint of superiority in his voice.

"Listen to what one of the finest textual critics said. This is a quote I found the other day from Dr. F. J. A. Hort." He walked to his desk and picked up several notepads and sorted them one by one until he found the pad he wanted. He flipped a few pages and began to read. "'In the variety and fullness of the evidence on which it rests, the text of the New Testament stands absolutely and unapproachably alone among ancient prose writings.'"

Rebekah rarely interrupted Dr. Aziz when he was in a flow of a thought, but she raised her hand, a conditioned response from school. She asked, "You just mentioned that the man you quoted, Dr. Hort, was a textual critic. What is that?"

"Well, Rebekah, this is the closest thing we have to science in our world of scholarship. You may have noticed how often I use words or phrases like probably, perhaps, nearly, we suppose, we guess, we suspect, and so on. As we briefly covered before, our world of philosophy and theology is not science. We certainly are not adversarial or opposed to our scientific brothers and sisters, but thoughts and ideas do not do well in formulas.

"But remember, while textual criticism is science, it is not necessarily an exact science. Let me explain. In a way it is quite ironic. One of the difficulties we have is that there are so many very good documents available. With thousands of texts available, how do we know which ones really represent the true thoughts of the original author? As I mentioned, there are no originals in existence; so all we have are copies, or more correctly, copies of copies. Some of the documents are entire books or letters, but many are only fragments. Do you begin to see the problem?" He did not wait for an answer.

"One other difficulty has to do with differences among the texts. Of all the documents in existence, no two are exactly the same. These differences are called variants. One of the imposing tasks is to sift through the available material and decide which variants most closely reflect the author's original meaning."

"Wait just a minute." Rebekah was now on the edge of the sofa, her eyes blazing. "Are you saying there are mistakes in the Bible? Over the years, Pastor Habib made it a point to say over and over again that the Bible was perfect without any error. He uses a particular word, but I can't remember what it is." Rebekah's black eyes were blazing with indignation.

"Sounds like I came just in time," Elisabeth said as she walked through the door.

"Elisabeth, did you know that your husband thinks there are errors in the Bible?" Her voice was filled with concern but not as intensely as her initial outcry.

Elisabeth set the tea tray down and began pouring the steaming drink. She neither looked surprised nor shocked at Rebekah's question. She gave Rebekah a faint smile. "Ishmael has always been honest in his studies and research. It has not always made him popular with some of his Christian colleagues. But listen to his explanations and when you have heard the full story, then you can decide what you think about it." She did not look up but continued to intently pour the tea.

Dr. Aziz stood quietly, teacup in hand, listening to the conversation. "Excuse me ladies, but if you don't mind, I would very much like to carry on with our discussion," he said with a glint of humor in his voice.

"Actually Rebekah, you are right on queue. You should see my seminary students react when we come to this point. I know without a doubt what they will say and how they will respond. It is very predictable. Tell me, Rebekah, when I said there are variants in the manuscripts, what primary emotion did it elicit?" There was a long silence. "Rebekah, this is not a rhetorical question; please give me a response."

"Well, I suppose anger was the primary emotion, followed closely by defensiveness," she responded.

"Very good. Again, you are well within the norm. This is often the response I get from the seminarians. But let me press on a bit. Why do you suppose the emotion was anger, not joy or sadness?"

"I am only guessing; but for me, when I believe something is true or right and someone challenges my belief, I get defensive. Besides, I have been taught the Bible is, oh I remember the word Pastor Habib used, "inerrant." If it is God's word to us, then why would there be mistakes in it? If there is one mistake who is to say that all of it isn't a mistake and..."

"Thank you, Rebekah. You have posed enough questions for the moment. And very reasonable ones I might add. I suppose my point is that you can see how difficult it is for humans to change once their minds are made up about something. For example, when people thought the world was flat it was difficult for them to consider any alternatives, even though mathematicians had speculated for centuries that the earth must be a sphere and calculated, to a high degree of accuracy, its circumference. While men thought it was flat, it deeply affected how they behaved. They were afraid to sail too far out to sea for fear they would fall off the edge." He moved his hand in a gesture of something going over the edge of his desk.

"For centuries the church taught and believed the earth was the center of the universe. God had made the earth special, so it must be the center, correct? It was not until several courageous men set forth their ideas to the contrary that the thinking began to change. If you remember, it was the church that attacked Copernicus and Galileo most severely, until they were proven right. But it still took many generations to change." Dr. Aziz frowned at the thought of such ignorance.

"The mind, Rebekah, is a powerful thing. Our belief systems determine our behavior and attitudes. So if we want to change man — truly change him — we must not concentrate on his behavior but upon his beliefs. That is what God does with us. When we come to Christ, we must lay aside our personal belief system and become submissive to God's.

"As He shows us His truth, we must change our lives and attitudes accordingly. Not just an outward behavioral adjustment, but also a heart change. I am afraid the church has not fully learned this. We still are focused on converts, which is the easy part, but not on making thinking disciples, which is the really hard work. But I am starting to preach now; let's get back to our topic." He turned and reached for his teacup sitting on the cluttered desk.

"Actually, rather than making us feel insecure or angry, the work of textual critics should be comforting. These critics are, for the most part, highly trained and skilled individuals who spend their lives trying to discern which documents best depict the original intent of the author.

"They are, as much as any scientist can be, objective researchers looking for the truth. They work under exacting controls. When there are variants, thorough and defined ways to find which is the closest to the original intent exist. It is a very sophisticated and complex methodology, so we can't discuss it in detail, but let me give you a couple of points." He looked around the room trying to find the black board, thinking he was in his classroom. He made a sweeping gesture with his hand and continued.

"When variants occur, the textual critic looks to two forms of evidence, external and internal, to try and find the best or most accurate rendering.

"Scholars differ as to how much weight one gives to the two forms, but the idea is that if one can get the best external evidence combined with the most accurate internal evidence, the result is a high degree of certainty.

"Oh, I forgot to explain what the two evidences are," Dr. Aziz said more to the air than to anyone in particular.

"Simply put, external evidence has to do with the quality and characteristics of the physical documents themselves. The documents found here in Egypt, for example, have been particularly good. Internal evidence has to do with the copyists and authors themselves. As a result of years of collecting data regarding a particular author's style, vocabulary, syntax, and other tendencies, the scholars become familiar with each author's characteristics. The good textual critics can read a portion of a text and know who wrote it. The Revelation of John, for example, is written in such poor Greek that a schoolboy today would be in serious trouble if he wrote Greek so poorly. On the other hand, the writer of Hebrews wrote in a beautiful, poetic, and fluid Greek that is quite exceptional."

Rebekah waited for Dr. Aziz to pause. "Dr. Aziz, you said 'the writer of Hebrews.' Don't you know who wrote that book?"

"Nobody knows for sure," he responded. It was never stated and history has lost the true identity. We can only guess. My personal opinion would be Apollos. His was an Egyptian Jew. But I don't know." He shrugged his shoulders.

The statement made Rebekah feel uncomfortable; but before she could say anything, Dr. Aziz was off again.

"Even the copyists had tendencies that are particular to each specific copyist. So, when the experts read the variant texts they can usually detect which writings are the mistakes caused by scribal habits and tendencies and which text is closest to the original intent of the author."

Rebekah's eyebrows pushed together. Her hands pressed against her forehead, elbows resting on her knees, head bowed. She felt exhausted.

"I don't mean to be rude," she said, "but is all this necessary? I asked fairly straight-forward questions about women in the Bible and what Paul actually meant in those passages. I thought you could tell me the answer in a few minutes. But I am afraid you are losing me. Does it have to be this complicated?"

Dr. Aziz walked over to her and gently put his hand on her arm. "Rebekah, as I told you in the beginning, this is a journey. For us, the journey is just as important as the destination. Many people just want answers without knowing the 'why.' But if you are ever to be the leader you believe the Lord wants you to be, simply knowing information and answers is not good enough. To lead well, you must know not only what you believe, but more importantly why you believe it.

"Like a skilled builder, I know that to lay a proper foundation is the most important thing we will do. We are laying the foundation that everything else we talk about will stand on. Trust me, my dear, it will all make sense when we finish." He moved back to his position by the window.

"Maybe I still don't understand why these textual critics are so important," Rebekah replied, sitting a bit more upright now. "What exactly do they do?" Rebekah looked at Elisabeth to see if she was equally confused. Elisabeth looked directly at Rebekah and smiled ever so slightly. Her head nodded as if to give Rebekah encouragement. "Do they actually translate the Scriptures?" Rebekah questioned.

"Well, now we are getting to the interesting part." Dr. Aziz took his glasses off and began to clean them with a tissue. "Textual critics are not primarily translators. They set the stage for the translators. In other words because this is such an exacting and tedious job, very few people are skilled and dedicated enough to do this full time. So, their job is to gather together the best texts that the translators use to make the translations. This text is filled with notations, footnotes, alternative readings inserted by the textual critics; all trying to give the translators the best chance of recreating the original meaning as clearly as possible." Dr. Aziz stood silently.

"So, if I understand this correctly, the textual critics go through the ancient documents and put together a text of the New Testament. Where there are variants they try to give information that the translators use to decide how to translate the passage most accurately. Is this what translators use today to translate the Bible?" Rebekah was now sitting more comfortably, leaning back on one of the sofa pillows.

"Precisely," he replied. "And therein lies a good deal of the confusion. The vast majority of the errors that occurred in the New Testament manuscripts came about during the first four hundred years. There were a number of reasons. First of all, the scribes who copied the letters and books had no idea that what they were copying was to become the Holy Scripture."

"As far as they were concerned, the documents were just letters sent to the churches and they were copying them to send them on, or making copies to take back to their own churches. Because of this, the copyist felt free to 'correct' or 'improve' places where the Greek was not proper or not clear. So they liberally changed verb tenses, words, and sentences. In many cases, they simply misspelled a word or used the wrong word. Their changes were perfectly understandable, but once a change was introduced by one scribe, the next copy contained not only the present copyists changes but all other changes made before. As a result, the accumulation of changes was passed on."

Rebekah was feeling tired; it seemed so late. But a glance at the clock on Dr. Aziz's desk showed it only seemed late. In a tired voice Rebekah asked, "Are you saying that most of the variants or mistakes were just a simple misspelling or using the wrong word? That seems pretty harmless."

"I did a little research yesterday and found that, according to Bible scholars, there are more than one hundred and fifty thousand variants.

Fortunately, fewer than four hundred affect the meaning very much and less than fifty have any real significance at all. The Holy Spirit did indeed guide and protect His word in a remarkable way.

"Another significant transition took place during the first four centuries of our era. Latin became the dominant language, and Greek began to lose its favored position. By 384 AD, when Jerome made the first 'authorized' translation, it was from Greek to Latin. This was referred to as the Vulgate translation. For the next eleven hundred years, the Vulgate was considered the primary source of scriptural text. But during that time there were many attempts to 'purify' Jerome's translation, thus adding more corruption to the text.

"I can see, Rebekah, that I have worn you out. I am sorry I went on so long, but this is so very important. You will see that when we come to addressing your concerns, however, this bit of the foundation will be crucial."

Chapter Nineteen

Every fourteen days Rebekah was on call in the emergency room at the hospital. She would come in at eight o'clock on Saturday morning and work a twenty-four hour shift. At first, she found the environment exciting and challenging, but over the years she had grown accustom to the shootings, the stabbings, car accidents, fights, the carnage of man.

Rebekah had finished the first twelve hours of her shift. It had been a busy evening; a bus had crashed into a tree, killing several people. Six were brought to her emergency room and the rest were sent to other hospitals. By the time she finished with the bus accident patients it was nearly midnight.

Rebekah sat in the doctor's lounge reading a medical journal, when a nurse opened the door and said, "Doctor, we need you in the emergency room."

Rebekah glanced at her watch; it was twelve twenty. She quickly walked the short distance to the emergency room where a nurse motioned for her to go into the examination room near the entrance. As she walked through the door and looked on the table, it took a second before she recognized what was lying there. The bloody mass was a young girl.

"What happened?" Rebekah whispered, the words barely audible.

The nurse looked up from the girl and responded. "We are not sure. Two street boys brought her in a few minutes ago. They said four policemen raped her, then stomped and kicked her. The boys were hiding in the same empty building where the attack happened, they saw everything. Apparently, when the policemen thought she was dead, they left. The boys saw her move slightly and carried her here. It happened a few blocks away."

"Where are the boys?" Rebekah asked.

"They were scared and ran out just shortly after I arrived." The nurse replied. "The boys wanted us to know that it was policemen that did it."

Rebekah stepped closer to the table. The child whimpered and groaned with each shallow breath. The beating had been so severe it was difficult for Rebekah to see any facial features. Arms and legs broken, chest crushed, head swollen to an ugly bloody mass.

The doctor part of Rebekah made a quick assessment; the girl was dying. There was nothing medically she could do; in a matter of minutes another young life would be gone.

The young girl looked up at Rebekah, one eye opened, the other had been smashed useless. The open eye was wild with fright and pain.

"Help me, please, help me," the girl whispered. A gurgling sound came from her chest.

Rebekah bent over to hear what the girl was saying. "I am afraid, please don't let me die. I am afraid. Help me. Please," she gasped through bleeding, broken lips.

Rebekah knew the situation was hopeless. She straightened up, removed the stethoscope from around her neck and laid it on the bed. Then Rebekah bent over once again and very gently put her left hand under the girl's neck, lifting her ever so slightly. With her right hand she tenderly stroked the girl's battered face. She placed her cheek against the girl's. Rebekah could feel the broken bones move under the skin.

Rebekah stayed in this position only a minute or two, until she knew the child was dead. Rebekah felt the weight increase ever so slightly as the spirit departed.

When she rose and looked at the nurse, blood was smeared on the left side of Rebekah's face. Her white coat blotched with dark red, bloodstains.

The nurse watched as silent tears rushed down Rebekah's cheeks. They looked at each other without a word; their mother-hearts knew Rebekah had done the right thing.

When Rebekah finished her shift, she had planned to go to church. But, exhausted and deeply troubled, she went home.

She lay on her bed wanting to sleep, but the image of the young girl's mangled body was too disturbing for her to rest. It puzzled her why she was so deeply affected. The earlier bus accident had been just as gruesome, seeing mangled bodies was certainly not new to her. Maybe knowing the death of this young child came at the hands of policemen — men who were supposed to protect citizens and uphold the law. Adults killing a child, the sense of injustice caused her stomach to tighten with anger.

Rebekah had been vaguely aware of the plight of the street children. Occasionally, they showed up at the hospital and ever so often at her clinic. Most cases she dealt with were HIV related. The statistics were staggering of the number of the street children who were infected. For the street kids, HIV was a gentle death, as they slowly wasted away. Most died in abandoned buildings and were discovered only when the odor of rotting flesh overwhelmed a passerby. Most were never discovered.

Rebekah felt sorry for the children, but it was more of an academic or professional concern than a personal one. But seeing such brutality inflicted on that helpless child kicked down all the walls she had carefully constructed to insulate her from the ugliness in the streets and the defenselessness of children who called the streets home. She wondered if this was an isolated incident or a way of life for these kids.

There was a good chance her son was living on those streets. She had hoped and prayed and believed, without reason, that he had found a nice family to love and care for him. There was no way of knowing, but the idea of her son living on the streets or maybe dying on the streets stabbed at her heart like a knife.

"We have to do something," she said out loud. Rebekah continued to lie on her bed thinking. If the police were indeed the ones who committed this crime, justice would never be served. But how many more times would this happen? How many more children would we be willing to sacrifice? How many more girls would have to die a brutal lonely death before someone does something?

Rebekah rose from the edge of the bed, changed her clothes, and went out. She knew that most of the street kids lived in the eastern part of the city. It was the poorest. Rebekah rode the bus to the general vicinity and started walking the streets. Having never been in this part of the city before she was not sure where to go.

Rebekah kept to the main street, walking slowly. She looked across the street and saw a long row of buildings; curious she made her way across the street and looked through the wrought iron fence. She could see many children. Some were running and playing games, others were sitting, talking in small groups.

Rebekah continued walking and looking through the fence. She eventually came to a large set of gates. Her heart started pounding for no reason; she felt a deep sinking feeling within.

She thought, perhaps, this was a private school. But the dilapidated buildings and the poor condition of the grounds made it look like a detention center. She noticed a sign on the fence. It was hard to read; the years and weather had not been kind to the lettering. As she came closer she began to make out the rusty words: Government Orphanage Number One.

Her mouth went dry; her breathing increased. She blinked several times to make sure she was reading correctly. She knew her son would be nearly sixteen by now, if he was still alive. And although it was a very remote chance, he could possibly be in there. Rebekah had often fantasized about being reunited with him. But it had only been a fantasy.

She reached forward and put both hands on the wrought iron bars and leaned closer. Rebekah stood and watched the children, the boys especially, to see if she might recognize her son. It was foolish she knew, but desperate mothers do foolish things.

Rebekah turned and walked away heavy-hearted. She spent the next several hours walking the trash-strewn streets, feeling a sense of urgency, but not knowing why.

A street vendor was selling cold drinks from a make shiftcooler packed with ice and mounted on two bicycle tires. It had two rusty handles sticking out that made it look like an overgrown wheelbarrow. The lady selling the drinks leaned on the top of the box looking away from where Rebekah approached. Rebekah asked for a Coke. She gave the lady a note and waited for change. As the lady fumbled through a handful of change, Rebekah asked, "Are there a lot of street children in this area?"

The woman looked her over shrewdly and replied slowly, "You are obviously not from the police or you would know the answer. What are you, a government worker?"

"No," Rebekah said. "I am a medical doctor and am curious about the kids living on the streets."

"You're curious, are you? Now that's a lot of help," she said dismissively.

"I am more than curious, I just don't know much about them. I am trying to learn," Rebekah said defensively.

"Well, you won't find many of them at this time of day. Come back tonight and they will be all over the streets. You won't have to look very hard." The vendor turned and walked to her chair and sat down waiting for her next customer.

Although Rebekah was weary, she did return that night. She was amazed at the transformation in just a few hours; it was like another world. People crowded the sidewalks and streets. Vendors were set up everywhere. As Rebekah waded into the human chaos her search for street children ended. They were everywhere.

Rebekah passed dozens of groups of children, some not more than five or six years old. The rest ranged from ten to sixteen or seventeen. Most were smoking cigarettes; some were sniffing glue from paper bags. Rebekah was both attracted to the youngsters and frightened by them. Some looked angry and mean, but most were just children acting like adults.

Rebekah wanted to stop and talk to them but felt foolish. What would she say? How would she start a conversation with a group of teenage strangers? She kept walking. Ahead of her was a group that seemed friendlier somehow. It was just a feeling, nothing more. They watched her pass.

Not knowing what to do or say, she stood in front of them for what seemed like several minutes. There were six of them: four girls and two boys. The girls made her feel safer. Three of the girls were leaning against a wall, the fourth sitting on the curb. One had a very short skirt the other three wore tight blue jeans, each wore oversized, white T-shirts hanging out. Two smoked the self-rolled cigarettes popular with teens, one other chewed a large wad of gum. None were pretty, they had lost any hope of beauty long ago and were content just to survive. The girls were young, maybe twelve or thirteen, the boys older. As Rebekah approached, they all turned to face her.

She stood before them silently trying to figure out what to say. Then one of the boys, with a swagger in his step, walked up to her. He wore a dirty baseball cap, jeans, and a cheap green shirt that had several buttons missing. His black skin glistened in the dim light. He was much taller than Rebekah and although he had a grin on his face, she felt uncomfortable.

"This is a little unusual," the boy said over his shoulder to the others. The girls laughed nervously. "But hey, whatever you like is okay with me."

Rebekah stood completely still, she had heard the words, but did not understand what the boy was saying. Before she could say anything, the boy continued.

"Well, which one do you want?" he said as he swung his hand out in a wide arch pointing to each girl.

"It's two dollars for thirty minutes." He leaned closer to Rebekah.

It took a few seconds before she realized he was offering one of the girls to her sexually. Her ears turned bright red; she flushed from head to foot with embarrassment. The harder she tried to maintain her composure the more flustered she became.

"Oh, no, you don't understand. That's not what I wanted at all," she blurted out.

The boy enjoyed watching Rebekah blush. "Oh, so you don't want one of the girls?" He was now looking at Rebekah in a leering and lustful way. "If you want to do it with me or my friend or both of us, we'll do it for free, for a pretty lady like you." He was now laughing, his friends jeering him on.

He suddenly grabbed Rebekah and drew her close and kissed her full on the lips. He was powerfully built and she could not push away. He finally released her. There were tears in her eyes. She was speechless.

Rebekah backed away from the group; they were laughing and pointing at her. The boy walked up to her and said in a very silky voice, "What are you going to do lady, call the police?" His face contorted into a scowl. He turned and walked back to the group.

Rebekah backed away a few feet further and then turned and ran as fast as she could. She bounced off people and pushed some aside in her effort to escape. She blindly jumped on the first bus to come, fortunately it was headed in the general direction of her flat. She exited the bus six blocks from her place. Once she made it back to her apartment, she was so shaken she could hardly put her key into the lock. Inside, she bolted the door and leaned against it. She was shaking and gasping for breath, great drops of perspiration drenched her forehead.

Chapter Twenty

The taxi driver swerved left to avoid an oncoming diesel truck carrying watermelons; he swerved right to miss a slow-moving pedestrian nearly clipping the basket on her arm. He cursed under his breath as a man in a business suit stepped back to let him pass. Rebekah tapped him on the shoulder and pointed. He immediately pulled over and she stepped out. She was late — again. The yellow-toothed driver smiled as he put the fare in the dirty visor above his head and pulled back into traffic.

Rebekah rang the bell and immediately the door opened. Dr. Aziz welcomed her and they walked to the study chatting about the events of the day. Dr. Aziz stepped to the left side of his desk to grab a note pad. He studied his notes briefly and began to speak.

"There is no doubt one of the greatest inventions of all times was the moveable type printing press in the early part of the sixteenth century. With the printing press, the kind of errors made by scribes was put to an end. This is very important. From then on, the inadvertent mistakes we discussed ended or at least could be more easily traced. But now we face a new set of problems.

"In 1516, Erasmus, the great Dutch thinker and humanist, edited one of the first printed Greek texts. This would be used for the next three hundred years as the basis for much of the New Testament translations. This is particularly unfortunate because these early editions were based upon the late Medieval Greek manuscripts, which were much inferior to the earlier ones. But hidden here, Rebekah, lies the answer to one of your questions.

"Pastor Habib is a wonderful man. I respect him greatly and he genuinely has a loving heart and a profound love for the Lord. We have been friends for more than forty years and have had many lively discussions. Unfortunately, he has fallen under the influence of good but misinformed teachers. In England, the translators followed the Greek text edited by a man named Robert Stephanus in 1550. This was the basis for the King

James Bible. On the European continent a few years later, after many revisions and editions, a standard text was presented. It was called the Textus Receptus, Latin for 'received text.' In the preface of this edition the editors declared: 'You therefore have the text which is now received by all, in which we give nothing altered or corrupted.' You see, Rebekah nowhere in the New Testament is there ever a claim that it is without error. The seed of this idea in modern times of the 'inerrancy of the word' can be traced to this statement made by the editors. And of course nothing could be further from the truth.

"As a matter of fact, in the late 1800s, the American Bible Society examined six different editions of the King James Version of the Bible and found nearly twenty-four thousand variants or differences in the texts. The King James Version is also known as the Authorized Version. Notice the term 'authorized.' By whom was it 'authorized?' By God himself or an ungodly king? For the next four hundred years, in the English-speaking world, this indeed became the much-loved and deeply entrenched standard translation. There is no doubt it was written in beautiful prose that was poetic to read. However, it was a poor translation.

"We are not going to go into detail here, Rebekah, but I will make some observations. During the last half of the nineteenth century and the first half of the twentieth, many new documents were discovered. These provided new textual data of all kinds confirming previous assumptions about some texts and refuting others. Research continued and science progressed so that by 1898, Dr. Eberhard Nestle presented a newly revised critical text. This text went through more than twenty-five editions and is still used today by Bible translators. While they may not be perfect, this is by far the best text we have ever had to create good translations."

Rebekah was unusually attentive and felt energized. She waited for Dr. Aziz to finish his sentence and quickly asked, "Does that mean that all Bible translations now use the same Greek text?"

"For the most part, yes," Dr. Aziz began.

Before he could continue Rebekah interrupted. "If they all use the same source in Greek how can there be so many different translations? Wouldn't they all be the same?"

"Now you have departed from the nice neat world of science and entered the world of art," Dr Aziz said with a chuckle, somewhat amused with himself.

"Art!" Rebekah exclaimed. "What does art have to do with it?"

"Well, translation is not so much a science as it is an art," Dr. Aziz muttered still amused with his own wit.

"Rebekah, remember at church when Dr. McKinsey speaks and someone has to translate for him? A good translator will not simply give a word for word translation, but will put what Dr. McKinsey means into thoughts that make sense to the listeners. Finding the right words or phrases that carry the correct meaning is really a fine art. When someone is particularly good, one hardly notices that the message is being translated at all. They speak with one voice. That is the sign of a good translator. We both know people who speak excellent English but who make very poor translators.

"The point, my dear, is that it is no easy task to translate from one language to another. It is especially difficult to capture not only the intent of the original language, but to then put it into meaningful and accurate words in a second language. This is the challenge of the New Testament scholars who attempt translation. Of course, the added problem is that nearly two thousand years have passed, so we have the dilemma of what is called historical distance."

"I have wondered," Rebekah said rather casually, "how the translators got it right. I know I prefer to read my English Bible rather than my Arabic Bible. I have noticed there can be a big difference between what the English and Arabic translations say. Are there some rules the translators follow?"

"Yes. There are many. But we are jumping a bit ahead. Because the task of translation is a formidable one and the expertise needed today is beyond one person, most modern translations are the work of committees. Basically, the hard work is to first understand the meaning of the original language and then communicate that idea using the best terminology in the so-called receptor language.

"If you translate it too literally it is stiff and does not read well. On the other hand, if you use a free approach and do not pay attention to the exact meaning of the original words, but pay more attention to the thoughts or ideas, you can end up with a paraphrase, which is not a translation at all. The best route to follow in my opinion is a middle way; this is called the dynamic equivalence. Here one tries to translate words, idioms, and grammatical construction to precise equivalents in the receptor language, but to do it in a style that is familiar to the modern reader."

"How do you know what is a good translation to use? I am not even sure I know what translation I have." Rebekah looked at Dr. Aziz as he stopped pacing near his desk. He pointed to a section of his bookshelves and said, "I have more than twenty translations there. Some are very good and some not. Generally speaking, I recommend using any of the modern translations as long as they do not paraphrase. In my opinion, the paraphrased versions take too many liberties."

Rebekah spent the next week looking through several translations she had borrowed from Dr. Aziz. She was fascinated to see how remarkably similar they all were. Except for a few words here and there, there were not many differences.

But she had to admit some passages were not all clear. Again she came back to her original question: How do we interpret God's word for today? Is there only one way to interpret certain passages? Her mind was racing ahead. She read the passages in Corinthians and First Timothy in several versions and they were still pretty clear. A woman was to be silent in church, in subjugation to men; the fate of women seemed firmly fixed no matter what translation she read.

The next week she was early for her meeting with Dr. Aziz. Her questions fueled during the week as she read and reread the portions of Scripture that were troublesome.

Dr. Aziz had his hand clasped behind his back, bending over looking closely at his notes lying on the desk. He straightened up, cleared his throat, and began to speak.

Rebekah blurted out, "Dr. Aziz, there is no hope! I have read these passages over and over and they are so clear: Paul forbids women from speaking in church; they must be in submission to men and may not have any leadership. Maybe we should just forget the whole thing; all the translations are the same. There's no hope."

The room was silent. Dr. Aziz walked slowly back to his desk, his head drooped slightly as he placed the notes gently on the well-worn desk pad. He took a deep breath, "Well, Rebekah, we have moved quite nicely along the journey over these many weeks. I guess this is as good a place as any to stop." Dr. Aziz tried to hide the disappointment in his voice, but Rebekah could hear it. "It is a pity, though; we have covered much ground that is not easily mastered and we are just ready to go to a higher plateau. The view from there is really quite interesting."

"But, Dr. Aziz, if the translations are accurate, which you said they are, then what's the use of continuing?" Rebekah said louder than she should have, her voice showing the hopelessness she felt deep within.

"We have only talked about one part of the process that leads to discovery, Rebekah. Translation is the half-sister to interpretation."

"Aren't they the same thing?" Rebekah challenged.

"Close, but no. Translation is putting the message from one language into another as accurately as possible. Interpretation is going back and finding out the meaning in the original and bringing it back to the present to see what it means today, here and now." Dr. Aziz paused and looked at Rebekah to see if she wanted to continue.

She put her backpack on the floor, reached for her favorite cushion, put it behind her back, and looked at Dr. Aziz. Rebekah smiled at him. This was the signal for Dr. Aziz to go on.

"Good. Before we can talk about interpretation, we must first understand the steps needed. The first task is to clarify what the original author intended to say to the particular group to whom he was writing. The question we must ask is, 'what was the original intended meaning?'" He jabbed the air with his finger.

"This is not an easy question to answer. It requires someone who not only knows the language, but also the historical setting, culture, political factors, topography, and any other particular and peculiar circumstances of the day. 'What did it mean then and there?' is another way of asking the question.

"Again, this is best done by highly-trained experts. Technically, this process is called exegesis. When we look at the passages that Paul wrote regarding the topic of women, we must do careful exegesis first. Another very important consideration in doing good exegesis is what is called literary context.

"Rebekah, what are words?" Dr. Aziz asked rather abruptly.

"I am not sure what you mean," she said, looking puzzled. "I suppose they are sounds that have a thought or idea connected to them."

"And by stringing several of these sounds together," Dr. Aziz continued Rebekah's idea, "we can express very complex concepts to one another. Rather remarkable when you think about it. By passing air over a set of vocal cords and making a particular sound, we communicate."

"We do this by associating ideas, concepts, and feelings with the words we form. A word by itself may or may not have much meaning; but when associated with other words, it takes on a specific connotation. Writing is similar, except we do not use sounds, we use symbols, called letters. But the meaning of the written words can only be understood in the context of the word written before and after; in other words in sentences.

"And individual sentences can be understood only in context of the preceding and following sentences. Here the main question is 'what is the point the author is trying to make?'"

"All this is very interesting," Rebekah interrupted, "but I am not sure I see what it has to do with interpretation." She tossed her head to one side as if that might help her follow Dr. Aziz's line of thought.

"If we do our work well and know what the text meant then and there, then we have a good chance of doing the next step well. It is called hermeneutics. It simply means taking the original meaning of the text and then bringing it forward some two thousand years and seeing how and if it applies to our lives today.

"It mostly involves common sense. But because language is fluid and words constantly change their meaning, we must always attempt to restate the meaning in today's terms. Most of the truths God wants us to understand are very clear and mean exactly the same today as when they were first spoken or written.

"When Paul writes that the wages of sin is death, it means the same today as when it was written. But in other cases, the message may have been solely for the people intended in the letter. For example, it is impossible to carry out Paul's admonition to greet the saints he mentions in Romans mainly because they have been dead for twenty centuries. So what to leave behind and what to bring forward is a basic question."

"What do you mean by 'leave behind?'" Rebekah asked with genuine concern. "Isn't that dangerous? Who decides what is important and what isn't? What happens if you ignore a very important point?" Rebekah challenged.

"Thank you, Rebekah, my dear. You have touched on some crucial issues. In a way, when we do hermeneutics, it opens up Scripture for man to make it say whatever he wants. So this is not primarily an academic exercise; it is a heart attitude. If we come to Scripture with a burning love for Jesus and a deep desire to obey His word and to love and encourage the saints, then we won't go far wrong.

"But if we come to Scriptures to justify an act or a point of view, we can manipulate them to say anything we want. Even when two lovely Christian folks read the same Scripture, they may go away with very different understandings. God seems to be okay with this; after all, it is not theology but love that is to be our signature.

"But just so I can feel like a professor I need to add that there are a couple of helpful rules that apply to hermeneutics. First of all, the text cannot mean what it never could have meant to its author or to the readers.

"This is why doing proper exegesis is so important. We can get into all kinds of problems and make Scripture say anything we want unless we are guided by this rule. In First Corinthians, Paul writes that 'when the perfect comes the imperfect will pass away.' Some have used this passage to say the gifts of the Spirit used by the early church are no longer necessary. Because the New Testament, the perfect, has now come, the imperfect gifts of the Spirit will pass away. "Therefore seeking to use the gifts of the spirit is wrong for today. This, of course, is one thing the passage could not have meant. Neither Paul nor his readers had any idea there would ever be any such thing as a New Testament. There is no possible way this is what Paul meant. So it cannot mean that today if it was never intended to mean that back then.

"The second rule goes something like this: whenever we share similar life situations with the first century setting, then God's word to them should also apply to us. Because of our shared human condition, whatever was written to them addressing these issues is applicable to us today and will apply as long as man is around.

"However, there are many passages that apply only to the specific situation of the first century and are not applicable today. For example, the eating of food offered as sacrifices at a pagan temple is not really an issue today. But it was a very serious issue when Paul wrote and was clearly understood by his readers in the early church."

"There is one further thing. In some portions of the text we simply do not know what was meant. Paul knew what he was trying to communicate and, most likely, those receiving the letter knew what he meant.

But we are left with our noses pressed against the glass looking in from the outside, not really able to figure out his intent. A great example is the passage where Paul writes: 'Do not be yoked together with unbelievers.' How do you take that, Rebekah?"

"As you know," she replied, "I am not married so this has always been one of those Scriptures I have taken very seriously — not to marry someone that is not a fellow believer. But I get the feeling you are going to question this."

"The problem lies in the fact that very rarely does the metaphor of a yoke ever refer to marriage in antiquity. So this is most likely not what Paul meant at all. The point is this, unless we are certain of the meaning, we need to be careful how we use it today to try to explain how God wants us to live. As a personal aside, common sense would tell us marrying a nonbeliever is not a wise thing to do, but we need to be careful not to use a Scripture out of context to try to prove a point."

Chapter Twenty-One

When Rebekah completed the several connecting bus rides and made the walk to Dr. Aziz's home, she was weary. Although she felt her time spent with Dr. Aziz was helpful personally, nothing much would change. What could she do to make any kind of difference? The whole world seemed to line up against her, in particular, and women in general.

Could no man learn anything from a woman in the church, simply because of the gender difference? Rebekah had just read a medical periodical. Of the contributing authors, twelve of the twenty writers were women. Why could women teach men in the world and not in the church? It just did not make sense.

No, there would never be any change. What difference would it make even if Dr. Aziz could pull some kind of magic trick and make the text say something different? Rebekah wasn't sure she cared enough any longer.

So she lifted a weary and heavy hand to the door. Elisabeth appeared with a warm smile and embrace and escorted her to the study.

"Ishmael is not here today." Elisabeth saw the worried look on Rebekah's face and hurried to explain. "He was called away. One of the international committees he serves on had an emergency, so he left for Geneva two days ago. But he asked me to give this to you."

Elisabeth walked over to the desk and picked up a large envelope and handed it to Rebekah. "Ishmael asked if you would read this while he was gone so you could continue the journey. He seemed concerned that you open it now and at least begin reading. I think he has a note for you inside."

"I will go and put the kettle on. Are you hungry, Rebekah? You always look so thin and tired. If you lived with us I would certainly put some meat on those bones," she said with a smile.

Rebekah smiled too. There was something about Elisabeth that

Rebekah loved. Maybe it was her human warmth — one knew she accepted them and cared for them. It wasn't said in words, but her spirit communicated her kindness.

"I wonder if Elisabeth ever struggles with the issues of women and her role in the church," she thought. "She seems content in what she is doing and, at least to me, her gift of serving others is meeting a very deep and personal need. And she is doing it without having to wrestle through the hard intellectual issues. Oh, how I wish I were like her! Life would be so much easier."

Rebekah turned the envelope over and released the clasp. She reached in and pulled out what looked to be about ten or fifteen pages of carefully typed pages. As she pulled out the papers a smaller piece of paper fell to the floor. She reached down and picked it up. It was a note written is Dr. Aziz's own scribbled handwriting.

There was an ink smudge on the top of the paper. It looked like it had been hidden in some old book and the outer margins had turned yellow with age. Dr. Aziz was famous for writing on anything, not necessarily nice pieces of stationery. One of his former seminary students, a friend from church, told Rebekah that Dr. Aziz gave an entire course from notes written on the back of used envelopes.

> Dear Rebekah,
>
> Please read this paper I wrote several years ago. It is on the place of women in antiquity. Very important that you get a perspective of what climate Paul was writing to. You will begin to see that Paul's view of women was nothing but revolutionary for his time. Do not be weary in well doing; God has a wonderful destiny for you. Keep steady.
>
> Regards,
>
> Dr. Aziz

She turned the papers over and at the top was a title written in capital letters. She began to read.

THE VIEW OF WOMEN HELD BY THE GREEKS, ROMANS, AND JEWS IN THE CLIMATE OF THE NEW TESTAMENT SETTING

It seemed Rebekah had only been reading for a few minutes, but it must have been much longer. When she looked up there was a pot of tea, a white porcelain cup, and snacks sitting on the table beside her. Elisabeth must have brought them in and, not wanting to disturb, left without a word.

Dr. Aziz's writing had so drawn her into first century life for a moment she was not sure where she was. Looking around, she saw the familiar desk and the comforting teapot; the books lining the walls were like tiny, friendly soldiers standing at attention, smiling down on her. In the hallway, light came from the kitchen.

"Elisabeth, are you there?" she asked raising her voice.

"I am here, Rebekah." Elisabeth's soft and comforting voice could be heard coming from the next room. Rebekah could hear Elisabeth's steps and she soon appeared in the hallway coming toward her.

"Are you all right, my child?" Elisabeth spoke as soon as she saw Rebekah standing by the sofa.

"I am not sure." Rebekah waited for Elisabeth to sit down beside her.

"Oh, Elisabeth, I wish I wasn't like this. I feel everything so strongly. When I see the poverty of our city, my heart breaks. When I see the children in my clinic come in with AIDS, my anger is almost uncontrollable. And I have such an intense desire to fight for things I see that are wrong, to speak out and stand against what I know are injustices.

"All it ever seems to do is to get me in trouble. I mean no disrespect, but I wish I were more like you. You seem so calm and content with your life. Is there something wrong with me?"

Elisabeth did not say anything for a long moment; then she burst out laughing. At first Rebekah was hurt, but Elisabeth quickly put her hand on her arm and said, "I told Ishmael the other day that you and he are from the same mold. You know, Rebekah, how much Ishmael likes you. You are not just another student. I think he sees in you a replica of himself.

"He was always getting into all kinds of trouble — more at the seminary than the university — because he hates the status quo. He must speak out, even if it is not popular. No Rebekah, there is certainly nothing wrong with you. God has made you one of his special people.

"As for me, there really never was much of an issue when I was a child. The role of the woman was strictly defined, end of discussion. I was never abused, my parents loved me, and I was content to live within the boundaries. I do not like change and I am quite happy with the status quo most of the time. So you can imagine when Ishmael and I first married, well, it was quite an adjustment." Elisabeth shook her head and smiled.

"But I came to see how wonderfully different God makes us all. He makes each one for His purposes. For you, Rebekah, you must be true to what God has called you to. You are a change agent, at least that is what Ishmael calls himself.

"I know he is thinking over his life, what he has done and what is left to do. He realizes his final years are at hand. And still he wants desperately to make a difference. I think he sees in you the change agent that he was not fully able to be. No Rebekah, there is certainly nothing wrong with you my dear."

"So what was so disturbing that you read in Ishmael's paper anyway?" Elisabeth inquired.

"Don't you read what Dr. Aziz writes?" Rebekah asked.

"In the beginning I tried; but to be honest, much of it was very academic and mostly boring. So now I just wait for Ishmael to tell me the general idea. But I don't think I've heard about this paper. You want to try and give me a summary?"

Rebekah looked at the papers in front of her, squinted her eyes, pursed her lips, and took a deep breath. She started speaking, softly at first. "I have always wondered how and why women were held in such low esteem in our culture. I thought it was just our customs, but now I see that this has been the prevailing view in most cultures. Apparently, from what Dr. Aziz says, in ancient times the dominant cultures of the Greeks and Romans had an incredibly low view of women. Just reading it makes me angry. Listen to this."

Rebekah began reading; her voice was low and steady. "Homer, the early Greek poet, set the stage for future Greek understanding of the role of women in the culture. Writing nearly eight centuries before Christ, he passed on the stories, myths, from earlier times. In his two major writings, The Iliad and The Odyssey, Homer laid the foundation for the ancient Greeks' world view.

"The way they interpreted their gods, their lives, and their cosmos for the next thousand years was given to them in these books. In

The Iliad, women were held in utter contempt. Homer blames them for being the cause of all malice, everything evil. They had no personal value, no personal identity, they were merely possessions to be used by men and then scorned.'"

"Listen Elisabeth to what Zeus, the supreme god says about how he would deal with his wife, Hera." Rebekah continued to read aloud.

"'I shall scourge thee with stripes.' Can you believe what Homer wrote? He is saying that the supreme god of the Greeks openly beat his wife. Dr. Aziz goes on to say that Zeus was sexually unfaithful and had children by many goddesses. If Zeus was to be the example for mere man, no wonder the Greek society had such a disregard for women. Homer went on to say that the place for women was strictly in the home and then given only very defined tasks."

"I had no idea," Elisabeth said.

"But it gets worse," Rebekah pushed on. "There was another Greek writer. Let me see if I can find it. Oh, here it is. Listen to this. 'The next important poet to be considered is Hesiod. His book, entitled The Theogony or Genealogy of the Gods, stated clearly that the origin of women was by Zeus as a terrible punishment. According to Hesiod, there was a time when men lived in wonderful bliss before women were created. Zeus, angry with Prometheus a fellow god for stealing fire from the Olympian gods and then sharing it with men, created a most heinous creature to punish the world. Her name was Pandora, the first woman."

"Can you imagine?" Rebekah's words were now filled with emotion. "The thoughts and ideas of Homer and Hesiod became the source of how Greeks thought about and treated women for more than fifteen hundred years. If our very origin was a curse from the gods, then why not treat us as subhuman creatures, with no dignity, no rights ... helpless little pests to be used by men with impunity?" Her blood was running hot. "That is just so ignorant."

Elisabeth looked at Rebekah's face and noticed that there were small veins protruding on both sides of her temples. Larger veins were pushing the skin along the side of her neck. Elisabeth didn't say anything but thought, "Rebekah has such a passion in her young soul. This must be what Ishmael so admires, a wonderful mind fueled by a fire burning deep within. But with that combination of gifts, pain and suffering will be her constant companion."

"It couldn't have been that bad," Elisabeth protested, as she adjusted the embroidered cushion next to her. "Surely Rebekah, there must have been some men who loved their wives and treated them kindly."

"Oh, I am sure there were some, but the idea that women were cursed by their very nature and only given by the gods to punish is an assumption that played itself out in real life. They became objects to be owned, totally at the mercy of men and punished at will. Elisabeth, don't you feel the despair?" Rebekah was looking intently at her friend.

"Didn't you say that was eight hundred years before Christ?" Elisabeth's voice showed genuine concern. "It must have changed over the years."

"Not according to what your husband wrote. According to his paper, the next important time was about 350 BC. There were three great Greek philosophers who had a major impact on Greek thinking of the day and remain major influences in philosophy even now."

"A man named Socrates was first. He discipled Plato who, in turn, mentored Aristotle. It appears that Aristotle was the teacher for Alexander the Great, who took Greek thinking and spread it throughout the world as he conquered nation after nation."

"They seem to have shared a common idea about women. Dr. Aziz quotes Plato as saying 'All those creatures generated as men who proved themselves cowardly and spent their lives in wrongdoing were transformed, at their second incarnation, into women ... In this fashion, then, women and the whole female sex have come into existence.'

"That doesn't sound like much progress to me," Rebekah said, the veins now disappearing below her youthful, smooth skin.

"But listen to what Aristotle has to say. He wrote that, 'the female was a monstrosity, a deformed male.'"

"He also wrote, 'The male is by nature superior and the female inferior, the male the ruler and the female the subject.' There we have it again, women were subhuman compared to men. Dr. Aziz writes that this was why, in many ways, the Greek culture turned out to be misogynistic."

"What does that mean?" Elisabeth asked.

"The word means the hatred of women. The Greeks actually came up with a word to describe the contempt they had for women. You never invent a word unless the idea is present first," Rebekah explained.

"What you believe determines how you act. Dr. Aziz points out that the consequences of their belief system were that women could not participate in any significant acts in society, no political activity; they were not educated, could not own any property or do any business. In essence, they had no higher status than slaves.

"State sponsored prostitution was initiated as early as 600 BC and fidelity in marriage was for the women only. Men were encouraged to visit prostitutes and have concubines. Wives were merely there to produce legal heirs, sons only, of course. When you think about it, many of the ideas of the Greeks are still with us." Rebekah's voice carried no anger, but there was a sadness that hung loosely on the words.

"Oh dear," Elisabeth sighed. "I think I need another cup of tea and maybe a piece of chocolate to soothe my nerves. You want some?"

"Just some tea please," Rebekah responded. As Elisabeth walked out of the room, Rebekah reread the section about the Romans. By the time Elisabeth returned with the tray of tea and chocolates, Rebekah was depressed.

Elisabeth poured the milk first, then added the tea as is required by British tradition. She handed the tray with the chocolates to Rebekah, who looked at the beautiful sweets and said, "Well, maybe just one," and smiled. They both knew neither of them would eat just one.

"What's next Rebekah, more bad news?" Elisabeth spoke as she returned to her place next to Rebekah.

"I am afraid the Romans were not much better. Dr. Aziz tells how, with the demise of the Greek military might, the Romans took over their role. By the time of Christ, the Romans ruled supreme, at least in the Mediterranean world. He describes the Romans as mostly brutes who ruled by force and discipline. However, they seemed to feel inferior to the Greeks in the matters of philosophy and culture.

"For the most part, it looks as though the Romans simply took on the Greek gods but gave them Roman names. A Roman poet named Virgil wrote a history of the Romans at about the time of Jesus. In his book, The Aeneid, he told mythical stories tracing the Roman beginnings back to tales told by Homer. It doesn't look as though the Romans changed the status of women. According to Dr. Aziz, while the Romans did not have the hatred toward women the Greeks had, they nonetheless thought of them in the same way — a sort of necessary evil. They still had no rights, no personal identity, and no individual name; parents simply feminized the father's name for the daughter.

"Also daughters could be discarded and left to die, except for the first born. A newborn daughter would be brought and laid at the father's feet. If he picked her up, she was kept. If he walked out, she was to be abandoned."

"We have friends from Switzerland," Elisabeth whispered. "They travel extensively. Recently, they visited us on their way back from China. The same thing happens all over China today. Female babies are left to die. What an incredible tragedy."

"I hate to say it," Elisabeth said rather abruptly, "but it doesn't look like there is much hope. Maybe this is our lot; maybe God did create us to be subservient. But I see what you mean about it being so unfair."

"I have not read all of the last part about the Jews. I could not read the bad news from three sources all together. I am getting tired Elisabeth, I think I'll go. When will Dr. Aziz be back?"

"I'm not sure, but come next week anyway. I'll have a nice dinner waiting for you and we can continue together. I'm getting more interested."

Chapter Twenty-Two

Elisabeth spent the afternoon in the kitchen. She loved to cook. It pleased her to see others enjoying her food, especially Rebekah. From what she surmised, Rebekah had neither the time nor the desire to cook for herself. So knowing her friend would get one good meal made Elisabeth's effort worthwhile.

Rebekah arrived right on time. She came directly from the hospital; she dropped her briefcase by the door, put her jacket on the hook, and walked into the dining room. The meal was already on the table. Rebekah loved Elisabeth's cooking.

"Thank you Elisabeth for fixing this wonderful meal. This has been a great week. I was on-call over the weekend, so I had some extra time. I continued reading Dr. Aziz's paper. Last week, I was so tired and discouraged that I could not read the part about the Jews. I started that section, but the beginning was just as bad as the Romans and Greeks. I could not bear to go on. But as I read the last pages, my heart nearly exploded with excitement."

"Was the Jewish idea of women that much different than the others?" Elisabeth asked.

"That is what threw me off last week. I began to read about the view the Jews had of women during Jesus' time. Dr. Aziz had several quotes from rabbinic sources. One said that each morning every Jewish man would utter a prayer saying something like, 'Thank you, God, that you have not made me a gentile, a slave, or a woman.'

"A Jewish man could divorce his wife for any reason. She was a thing to be possessed, not a person. Women, like in the Roman and Greek worlds, were blamed for much of the evil, especially sensual temptations. One quote said something about women being evil and easily overcome by a spirit of fornication. So, once again, it was the woman who was to blame."

"That doesn't sound very good. What made you so excited?" Elisabeth inquired.

"It wasn't like this at the beginning. Dr. Aziz showed that over the years the Jews added many laws in interpretations to those laws. These accumulated teachings eventually produced books of themselves like the Mishnah and Talmud that became the codification of the original word of God. The Jews eventually began to use these additions to the original word of God with equal value. This is one reason why Jesus was so angry with the Pharisees and Sadducees. They had corrupted and distorted God's word with man's laws. They ended up not being any better off than the Romans and Greeks, although they thought they were.

"Dr. Aziz included a study of the first chapters of Genesis. He made several wonderful observations. Elisabeth, you must read for yourself. I cannot remember all the details, but the idea was that a loving God made a creation that He loved and cared for. One thing I remember is that God said, after every creation day, that it was good. After He made man, God said, This is not good, something is missing. The good thing that was yet missing was woman. That is so encouraging.

"Next, was a description of how woman was created. Dr. Aziz referred to it as a shared origin. God did not make woman from the dust of the earth, but directly from man of the same substance. So woman was not lesser in any way from man."

"Would you like anything else to eat, you have been talking and haven't eaten much." Elisabeth sounded a bit irritated. "If God created man first, doesn't it mean that, because woman was created second, that she is not his equal?" Elisabeth asked as she poured more water into Rebekah's glass.

"That was one of the points Dr. Aziz made. He said if that line of thinking were true, then the snakes and rabbits and all the creatures made before man would be higher than man. He states that just the opposite could be argued. It seemed that God was making His creation in order of significance, from least to greatest. Woman was created last, so it could be argued she was the greatest of creation. I like this thinking a lot," Rebekah exclaimed, a mischievous smile on her face.

"Before you get too many crazy ideas in your head, Rebekah, it also says that woman was created to be man's helpmate. Doesn't that infer she was created to be a helper, not an equal?" Elisabeth was now standing, stacking the empty plates.

"You have got to read the paper. Dr. Aziz addresses this as well. I don't remember the Hebrew phrase he used, but his argument said that the meaning of the Hebrew word for helper was not someone sub-servient, but refers to someone more capable, more powerful, more intelligent. The Psalmist used the same word when he talked about the Lord being his helper. It means someone stronger helping someone in need. I cannot remember the rest, but it is so important. Wait here and let me get the paper from my briefcase."

Elisabeth carried the dishes into the kitchen as Rebekah strode down the hall to retrieve the research. Rebekah came back smiling and sat down at the small, wooden kitchen table. Elisabeth made another trip to the dining room to pick up the remaining serving plates. When she returned, Rebekah was reading. Elisabeth began washing the dinner dishes.

"Here's the second part. Dr. Aziz says that the second word of the Hebrew phrase means equal. In other words, the phrase could be restated to say 'God made for Adam an equal helper, to work with him, not for him.' Elisabeth do you see how important this is? We are no longer mere servants but co-workers. That is so liberating. It is like a huge weight has been lifted.

"Dr. Aziz also points out that God addresses them both ... 'let THEM rule over ... all the earth. God blessed THEM and said to THEM, be fruitful. They originally had joint and equal leadership. Genesis One and Two set the original intent of God for man and woman as equals, ruling together over God's creation." Rebekah put down the papers and looked intently at Elisabeth. She turned from the sink with a dishtowel in her hand, carefully drying a plate. She saw Rebekah's look of excitement.

"Rebekah that is truly amazing, but what went wrong? Wasn't it the woman who sinned first and then dragged her husband down?"

"That is what I had thought as well. I am not sure where I learned it, probably in church. But Dr. Aziz makes it very clear that the Genesis story includes both the man and the woman in the fall. He says that the Hebrew is very clear when it uses the plural and when it is singular. In English, we must know the context to know if it is singular or not, but in Hebrew there are actually two different words.

"It is absolutely clear when the dialogue was occurring between Satan and the woman, Adam was there. When Satan said 'you,' he used the plural word, both were there. Eve also replied in the plural. After she had eaten, she turned and gave it to Adam, 'who was with her and he ate.' So even here, it was not the woman alone who sinned, they did it together." Rebekah was busy shuffling the papers. She was looking for something.

Elisabeth walked over to the table and pulled the small wooden stool out just enough so she could sit down. "But didn't God curse the woman for her sin ... after all, it was her fault?"

Rebekah looked up from the papers and replied, "That is what I was led to believe, but this research shows that it is not true. God cursed Satan and the ground, but to man and woman He merely explained the consequences of their action. It is very interesting, however, that God did say that there would be a special hatred that Satan would have for the woman.

"Maybe that could explain the universality of the plight of women. This world is still Satan's domain and he has a special hatred for women; so perhaps the universal subjugation of women is Satanic in nature. But it is also true that in the very same passage, God gives the first hint of the redemption to come, through a woman." Rebekah sounded triumphant.

While Rebekah continued to teach, Elisabeth reached over and picked up her well-worn Bible from the edge of the table next to the wall. Rebekah noticed how worn the pages were. She also noticed how lovingly Elisabeth held God's Word in her hands — a very real sense of reverence.

It suddenly dawned on Rebekah; she had never been in the kitchen before. They had always met in either Dr. Aziz's study or the living room or, like tonight, in the dining room. Rebekah felt a little uncomfortable. She did not know how she knew, but this small room was Elisabeth's private sanctuary. This was the place Elisabeth read her Bible and prayed for her children, Dr. Aziz, and most likely for her.

Rebekah looked at Elisabeth's hands that gently held her Bible. They were wrinkled and worn, yet tender and kind. They had once been beautiful, soft, and young, but time had made its mark as it always does. Still, there was something special about Elisabeth's hands. Rebekah knew it the first time her friend had gently touched her arm that night she had told them both her awful secrets. They were hands that brought blessing and healing, comfort and warmth, love and acceptance. "I want my hands to be like that," Rebekah thought.

Elisabeth was carefully turning the pages of her Bible, then stopped. She read silently for a moment and said, "What do you think it means when God tells Eve that 'your desire will be for your husband and he will rule over you?' That's chapter three, verse sixteen."

"That's a good question; I don't know. I am making a list of questions to ask when your husband returns. I'll add that to the list. Maybe it has to do with the nature of redemption."

"Was there anything else Ishmael wrote that was interesting?" Elisabeth asked. "You obviously liked what he said about the origin of woman?"

Rebekah was still looking through the papers and spoke as she looked up. "He devoted a couple of pages at the end to the way Jesus dealt with women and showed how revolutionary it was, especially compared to the other so-called great thinkers and leaders up until his time.

"The Greek philosophers were women haters. The Roman leaders used women as objects and the Jewish religious leaders despised women, yet Jesus treated them with dignity. I had not noticed it before, but since reading Dr. Aziz's paper I read several of the gospels looking for specific incidents of Jesus' encounters with women. It was a truly revelational experience. Listen to some of what I found." Rebekah's voice had the familiar enthusiasm.

"There did not seem to be any exclusivity in Jesus, he came to minister to both men and women. He came as the answer to the fall of man, to restore both men and women to their rightful place. To the woman caught in adultery and brought before Jesus, there was not only compassion but also much more. It was clear that the Pharisees were hypocritical. Where was the man who was the other partner in the act? He had been let go; yet the Old Testament makes it clear that if two are caught in adultery, then both should be stoned.

"The most obvious fact is how corrupted the Jewish leaders had become. Dr. Aziz points out that this passage later became so offensive that some of the ancient manuscripts intentionally left the story out. I noticed when I read the account in the Gospel of John that there was a line across the page and a note saying that many manuscripts do not include this account. But what Jesus was doing was establishing equality for men and women. Sin was sin, regardless of gender.

"I also noted what Jesus said about divorce. Previously I had been confused regarding this subject. But I think I now see what Jesus was really saying. According to this paper, the Jews were not much different from the surrounding cultures when it came to divorce. Any man could divorce his wife for any reason; how they went about doing it was a bit different, but the idea was the same. But a woman could not divorce her husband for any reason; she had no rights.

"Jesus revolutionized the thinking by suggesting that women had the same rights as men. Elisabeth, look up Mark chapter ten, verse ten. It is amazing, Jesus said very clearly the reason for the divorce laws was because their hearts were hard. Then he went on to say, well, read it."

Elisabeth found the verse and began reading: "Anyone who divorces his wife and marries another woman commits adultery against her. And if she divorces her husband and marries another man, she commits adultery."

"See what I mean, Elisabeth? Jesus is not necessarily answering the legal question about divorce, but is saying that the rights of the woman are the same as for a man. No wonder the Jewish leaders hated him.

"I know it is getting late; but let me share one more observation. I do not know if these are valid or not, but I don't think I am too far off — at least I hope I'm not. In the Gospel stories, there are many accounts of women learning directly from Jesus. Remember Mary and Martha? It says that Mary was sitting at Jesus' feet while he was teaching the disciples, and later when Martha was complaining of getting no help, Jesus said Mary had chosen the better thing. So Jesus tore down the barrier of women not being worthy of education. You can imagine what the Pharisees thought when they heard that Jesus was teaching women!" Rebekah said excitedly.

"I also noted that there were at least seven women to whom Jesus ministered. Dr. Aziz gave me the clue; the paper stated that the Greek verb to minister is "diakoneo." He gave the references in the Gospels and I looked them up. It is used in exactly the same manner in the Gospels when talking about women as it is used in the book of Acts when talking about men. So there was no difference; Jesus himself set the standard of what women can do. Nowhere did he restrict their participation because of gender."

Elisabeth laid her Bible on the table. She was flipping the pages, stopping to occasionally lick her finger so she could turn one page at a time. She stopped at a certain page and looked at Rebekah. "I think what you are saying is very interesting Rebekah; but all accounts of the Gospels list the names of the disciples and I do not see any women listed. Doesn't that mean that only men can be the leaders in the church?"

"I have thought about that myself. It is another one of the things I want to talk to Dr. Aziz about. But when you look at it reasonably, what does that really say? All of Jesus' disciples were not only men, they were all Jews. They were all Aramaic speaking. They were most likely all, or at least mostly, uneducated and illiterate. One was a traitor and thief. Most were self-serving bigots to start off with.

"So, if you follow the line of reasoning that Jesus only picked men to be leaders, you must also include the other characteristics as well. So what you find is that only male, Jewish, Aramaic-speaking, uneducated, self-serving bigots can be in church leadership. And while, except for the Jewish, Aramaic speaking part, this may very well be the case in the church today, I don't think that is what Jesus had in mind."

They both looked at each other for a moment and burst into laughter. "Oh, Rebekah, you are so very naughty. That would have been something Ishmael would have said — only he would have said it to the elder board!" They both continued to smile enjoying their private humor.

Chapter Twenty-Three

The walk from the bus stop to Dr. Aziz's flat was beautiful. Rebekah noticed the flowers blooming in people's small gardens. The air was warm and fresh, certainly not always the case in a city of more than twenty million people. But this was a fantastic evening; the familiar smells were invigorating. She was also excited to see Dr. Aziz once again. So much had happened since her last visit. There was so much to talk about. She was a little concerned that some of her conclusions would not be accurate, but in a way that was not so important anymore. She felt that she was coming closer to the truth ... not her truth but God's.

Dr. Aziz opened the door. Rebekah was so happy to see the bright smile and twinkling eyes that welcomed her. They made their customary stroll to his study and chatted about his trip and her week at work. Elisabeth prepared the refreshments and sat next to Rebekah.

"Elisabeth tells me you have had quite a good time of discussion in my absence." Dr. Aziz looked pleased. "So tell me, Rebekah, how would you summarize these past weeks' thinking and discussions?"

"It is all about redemption," Rebekah said without hesitation.

Dr. Aziz's eyebrows shot up involuntarily. He was sitting in his brown swivel chair; the leather on the arms had long since decayed. He turned toward his desk and grabbed a writing pad. "Go on, Rebekah, I just want to make some notes."

"It all has to do with redemption," she repeated. "At first, I thought it was about injustice, inequality, bigotry, and cultural bias. But over the past weeks, as I read the Bible with a new perspective, I began to see that God wants to restore men and women to their rightful places. Genesis One and Two are full of God's original intent. After man fell in sin and disobedience, he was displaced and had to wait all those years for Christ to come.

"If I understand redemption correctly, it is God's purpose, through the work of Christ on the cross, to restore us to the place of fellowship and relationship with Him. But secondarily, it was to restore mankind to his original position of relating to one another. And perhaps third, to give mankind the authority he had originally been given over the earth that Satan took away. I am not so sure about the last one, but I am convinced about the first two. I was particularly intrigued by what Jesus said about the world to come, the afterlife. Every indication that I can find is that there will be no gender distinction whatsoever."

"That is very interesting, Rebekah. I do not recall ever having a student make that connection before. They all would argue along the lines of justice or roles or equality, but you are absolutely correct. The basic issue is: what is the nature of redemption? What did God intend through it? It seems to me that what we have today in the church is partial redemption. Men can be fully restored, but not women. I think you are on to something." Dr. Aziz leaned back in his chair and thought for a long moment.

"I am very happy with the progress you and Elisabeth," he paused here to look at his wife and give her a warm smile, "have made over the past weeks. But we still have some work to do. The apostle Paul wrote some difficult passages. If it is any encouragement, even the apostle Peter said that Paul wrote things difficult to understand, and he was there!

"In many ways, reading Paul's writings are like listening to one end of a telephone conversation. If you are in the room listening to a friend talk on the phone, you can only hear what that person is saying. You must guess at what the other person's questions or statements are by the tone of voice and what is being said in response. This is how it is with Paul's letters.

"In every letter, Paul is answering questions from churches or individuals. We do not know what the questions are exactly; we have no record of them, so we must guess based on what we know of the culture, setting, and circumstances of the day. It is also extremely important that we compare what Paul said with what he wrote to other churches. He would not have given one church strict guidelines and a different set to another church.

"We must also compare Paul's writing with the words of Christ to make sure they harmonize. One reason we have no record of the questions is because everyone in the church knew what the questions were, so keeping record of them was not important. They came to ask Paul personally what they should do in a particular situation. He would then dictate a response to a scribe who would write his reply. He did this so the church receiving the letter would know this is what he said and not simply the report of the people sent to inquire. We must read his letters carefully and do our exegesis properly in order to find out Paul's original intent.

"Now, the reason these are called 'problem passages' is simply because they bump against other passages that Paul wrote. In other words, Paul seems to be contradicting himself. We know Paul is too clever for that, so how does one reconcile the various statements?

"On the trip, we were not in meetings the entire time, although it seemed like it some days. When I had a bit of free time, I did a brief survey of the New Testament and listed all the places where Paul seemed to recognize women's role in the church. This is not an exhaustive list, but will certainly be representative of his overall view of women ministering within a church setting. The reason this is so important is we are putting in place a clear standard to which we can compare what Paul says in other places.

"The primary example is Priscilla, sometimes known by her nickname, Prisca. If you read Acts, you find that she and her husband, Aquila, were goods friends with Paul. They worked at the same trade, were exiled from Rome and helped Paul plant the churches in Corinth and Ephesus.

"There is no doubt they were instrumental in Paul's ministry. Paul speaks of them as colleagues and faithful co-workers. Not just Aquila, but both. As a matter-of-fact, it is most unusual that whenever Paul mentions them he refers to Priscilla first. This was not normal in the Greek and Roman culture. The man's name always came first. Always!

"This unusual sequence made me curious, so when I returned home I did a bit of research and found a very interesting quote from John Chrysostom, one of the early church fathers who lived in the fourth century AD. Writing about Priscilla he said ... let me get the quote." Dr. Aziz reached over to his desk and picked up one of the writing pads.

"Here it is. This is by a man not known for much sympathy toward women. 'This too is worthy of inquiry, why, as he addressed them, Paul has placed Priscilla before her husband. For he did not say, "Greet Aquila and Priscilla," but "Priscilla and Aquila. He does not do this without reason, but he seems to me to acknowledge a greater godliness for her than for her husband. What I say is not guesswork, because it is possible to learn this from the Book of Acts. Priscilla took Apollos, an eloquent man and powerful in the Scriptures, but knowing only John's baptism, she instructed him in the way of the Lord and made him a teacher brought to completion.'

"It is clear that the great Apollos had a woman instructor. Even Tertullian, another early church father who certainly did not promote women, has said, 'by the holy Prisca the Gospel is preached.'

"The next woman on our list is Chloe from the church in Corinth. Paul refers to her in First Corinthians chapter one, verse eleven. '... some from the Chloe's household have informed....' Now the word household is not actually in the Greek. Paul uses what is called an ellipsis. Let me explain. In English and most other languages, we say, 'I am going to church, so is Rebekah.' The ellipsis would ask the reader to understand that Rebekah was going to church also.

"But if you just read, 'so is Rebekah,' by itself it would make no sense. But by the context of the preceding phrase, the statement is clear. Paul uses the exact same wording in Romans sixteen, when he says 'greet those ... of Narcissus, greet those of ... Aristobulus,' the actual words "of the household" are understood. These greetings to Narcissus and Aristobulus are normally taken to mean those who lead the house churches. The implicit understanding is that Paul was using this greeting to signify certain house church leaders and Chloe was part of this group. If Chloe was leading a house church, then it makes sense that a delegation from her house church was asking Paul for specific instructions.

"Phoebe is the next one on my list. She was associated with the church in Cenchrea, a small town just outside of Corinth. While we cannot be sure of her exact standing in the church, Paul most certainly held her in high esteem.

"At the very end of Paul's letter to the church in Rome, chapter sixteen, Paul gives many greetings to his friends. But he starts off by commending Phoebe, our sister a "diakonos." Remember this word has been translated as servant, deacon, and sometimes minister. It is exactly the same word Paul used to describe any of his male co-workers. The King James Version feminizes the term and makes it deaconess; however, there was no feminine form of this word in Greek at that time and there simply is not a distinction of the role of minister and deacon in the New Testament.

"So, she was a minister of the church in Cenchrea. This is the only time in the New Testament that the noun "diakonos" is modified by the phrase 'of the church.' I have just one more point to make; I wanted to know exactly what the word meant to be a helper. I know Greek well, but this word was not familiar to me. When I looked it up, I did not recognize the meaning. This word, "prostatis," is only used once in the New Testament. It can mean helper but only in a secondary sense. Its primary meaning is more a servant-leader; it is a leader who champions the cause of others rather than pursuing self-interests.

"Paul qualifies Phoebe as not just a participant in the church, but as one in a role of leadership. So what Paul is saying to the church in Rome is, 'this is a very important lady, give her a reception that is worthy of her status in the church.'

"To finish the list of names in Romans sixteen, the most interesting is Junia. Paul referred to Andronicus and Junia as apostles, his relatives, fellow prisoners, and believers in Christ.

"Now listen to this Rebekah, I can find nowhere in antiquity where the name Junia is anything but feminine. I checked with several textual critics and there is every reason to believe that the original is Junia. In later manuscripts, the name Junias is found, which is the masculine form. Nowhere in all of history is Junia used for a male except in the New Testament. Why do you think that is?" Dr. Aziz waited for an answer.

"Could it be that later on when the church was more influenced by the culture or other early thinkers that a scribe could not believe that a woman could be an apostle and changed the name and made it masculine?" Rebekah responded.

"Exactly," Dr. Aziz said excitedly. He was now in full stride, pacing back and forth across his small study. "The best texts all say Junia, but even today many translations try to make it a male name. I looked at seven modern translations; three translate it as Junia and four as Junias. So you see the prejudice did not end with the scribes. You can imagine the implications if there was a woman apostle. This alone would provide proof that women did and should be allowed to serve in any office if they have the talents, gifts, and calling."

Rebekah had never heard Dr. Aziz speak so directly. He was the careful scholar, always couching his remarks in terms that never seemed to put him in a fixed position but not today.

"Dr. Aziz you seem adamant about this. I don't recall ever hearing you speak so definitively on any subject thus far, especially something as controversial as this subject. Has something happened?"

Elisabeth joined them and only heard the last part of Rebekah's comment. "Are you getting yourself into trouble again, Ishmael?" Elisabeth asked with a wry smile.

"Well, that is a good observation, Rebekah. We scholars are very much like herd animals. We seem to run in packs; we like to be a part of the whole. In a way it offers protection. We certainly do not get rich or famous doing what we do, so the main thing we want is the respect of our fellows. While we might fight and fuss amongst ourselves, arguing over the slightest detail, we generally accept one another and live in harmony.

"If a maverick comes along and sticks his head up above the rest or goes completely against convention, then the worst thing happens to him — he is ostracized. That is the kiss of death professionally. So most of us are conditioned to keep our heads down to stay safe. Do you see what I mean, Rebekah?"

"Are you saying that you can't come up with anything new for fear that you will labeled as a maverick and put out of the herd?" Rebekah sounded skeptical.

"Not exactly. If you discover a new truth or even a new angle on an old truth and do not present it in the right way, carefully couched in the proper terminology, others may feel up-staged or threatened. Or, they may simply think you are trying to draw attention to yourself. So you remain quiet or write it up and then publish after you die. That may be one reason why theology generally lags behind the culture and fails to address the social issues of the day. We certainly do not move quickly.

"In many ways, this is healthy. We theologians feel we have a divine responsibility to protect the truth of Scripture, so we are very hesitant to accept new ideas or change without a great deal of thought and discussion.

"On the one hand this can be to our own detriment. I remember studying at university during the time of the civil rights movement in the U.S. I longed for the church leaders to speak out, to take the lead in fighting the injustice, bigotry, and discrimination. But they stayed silent. So the activists, the politicians, and radicals did what the church should have done.

"Is it any wonder we are considered irrelevant by our society and culture? Not many of the theologians spoke up for change, although if anyone should have known the Scripture and what it said, it would be them. Instead, many continued to use Scripture to fight against equality for the minorities, the blacks in particular. To be honest Rebekah, I have not been any different."

Dr. Aziz's voice was suddenly lower and filled with emotion. He turned in his chair and faced the window, slowly reached into the side pocket of his navy blazer, and pulled out a handkerchief. With his back to Rebekah and Elisabeth, he wiped tears from his eyes and blew his nose loudly. Rebekah looked at Elisabeth; she simply shrugged her shoulders as if to say, "I don't know what's going on either."

After a long pause, Dr. Aziz turned back around in his chair, his voice once again controlled. "Please excuse me, but this has become a very emotional issue for me. When you first started coming over Rebekah, I thought this would be a pure exercise in academics, but something has happened, though I am not sure what. I somehow feel so deeply the pain of the oppressed. If I keep this up, Elisabeth will need to buy another set of handkerchiefs. Now, where were we?"

Rebekah spoke up. "We were talking about Junia. I was wondering if it is really that important if Junia turned out to be a woman apostle?"

"It just might be, at least it will be for some." Dr. Aziz sat silently for a long while. Then, as if the conversation never happened, he started on.

"Euodia, Syntyche, Priscilla, Mary, Persis, Tryphena, and Tryphosa were all women that Paul referred to as either his co-workers or fellow laborers, using exactly the same words that he used for any male." Dr. Aziz laid his writing pad on the desk and picked up another one from the top of a stack.

"Whatever we look at from here on must be viewed in light of what we have already laid down. So what were the problems? I have been looking at the so-called 'problem passages' and have divided them into three basic categories. The first category has three issues: submission, authority, headship. Next is women keeping quiet in the church. And finally women teaching in the church. When we get together next time, we will begin talking about these topics."

Chapter Twenty-Four

Rebekah was angry for sometime after her first encounter with the street children. She had only wanted to help. But instead of being appreciative of her intentions, they had jeered and laughed at her, humiliated her. She would never go back.

When she told Elisabeth and Dr. Aziz about the incident, Elisabeth put her arms around her and consoled her. Dr. Aziz said nothing, but Rebekah knew from the look in his eyes that he had plenty to say and would when he was ready.

Almost a month after her first attempt at contacting the street kids, Rebekah was having lunch with a friend. She told her friend about the incident on the street; how silly she felt, how utterly humiliating it was. Yet something within would not allow her to stop her pursuit. Rebekah confessed she had no idea of what to do.

Her friend, who also came from the Hartford School, looked at Rebekah strangely, "Do you remember Helen? A year behind us. She is now a social worker, helping the street children. You need to call her."

Rebekah felt excited yet uneasy. As soon as her friend mentioned Helen's name something sparked within her. Rebekah had a premonition that her life was about to take on a new direction; goose bumps raced up her arms.

Rebekah remembered Helen from school. Helen was not in her group of friends, but there was a bond between most of the girls that shared a common Hartford experience. It took many calls to find Helen's telephone number. When they did connect, they decided to meet at Helen's office.

The building that housed the offices for Human Services was a dreary old structure standing in the heart of the city. On the fifth floor was the Department of Social Welfare. Each tiny office held four workers. The desks were crammed back to back; there was barely room to walk between them.

Rebekah could not find the correct room and had to ask someone where Helen's office was. As she walked into the room, Rebekah was stunned at the sheer amount of files and folders stacked on each desk. Helen's desk was furthest from the door. There was only one other worker in the office so Helen offered Rebekah a seat at the desk across from her.

Helen was a tiny young lady. Her dark hair was cut square in the front and then cropped short around to the back. The cutter tried to make the hair come out even at the back, but one side was longer than the other. Rebekah suspected Helen was the cutter. She was not pretty but not ugly, just very plain. Nothing about her was particularly noticeable. She spoke in a high-pitched, whisper of a voice. Rebekah caught herself leaning forward so she could hear Helen speak.

Rebekah explained in some detail what had happened over the past months, of her increasing interest in trying to help but not knowing how. Rebekah finished by saying, "Helen, can you tell me how can I help?"

Helen said nothing; she was looking through some papers on her desk. Finally she picked up a paper, looked it over, and said, "We are overwhelmed. We never have enough money or people. This United Nation's report came out just a few weeks ago. It estimates there are one hundred and fifty million street children in the world. Of these, about forty percent are truly homeless, parentless children."

Helen handed the paper to Rebekah. "The rest spend their time on the streets but have a parent or place to go. In many cases, the ones who move full time into the streets come from these very poor families where abuse and brutality are common. Cairo is about in the average. We have a population of approximately twenty million; there are between one-half million and three quarters of a million street children. Some are as young as three or four years old."

Rebekah was reading the report and listening to Helen at the same time. Both sources of information where beyond comprehension. "What do you do to help them?" Rebekah asked quietly.

"To be honest, not much. It is not just our problem; every country in the world is facing the same dilemma. Where there are large populations of street kids, the crime rate is high, the incidences of AIDS is epidemic; drugs, prostitution, you name it, it's there." Helen folded her hands in her lap.

Rebekah waited till the other worker left the room. Then she leaned over the desk and said very softly, "The kids who brought in the young girl said four policeman raped and beat her to death. Can that be true?"

Helen's dark eyes darted around the room, she looked at the door for a long time to make sure no one was coming near. "There have been reports that the government has used soldiers to cleanse the streets of the children. Two years ago, the government hosted a world trade conference; they did not want to be embarrassed by all the street kids hanging around the hotels and tourist areas. In the immediate vicinity of hotels and meeting venues, the soldiers rounded up several hundred street kids. They were supposed to take them across town and let them off. But for many days and weeks afterward, bodies were found floating in the river. Fifty bodies were found in a shallow grave just on the outskirts of town."

Helen continued hurriedly. "The police get frustrated. There are so many kids and they are almost all doing something illegal. Sometimes the police just want to scare them. So, yes, the police do take their anger out on the kids. It does not happen every day, but it is not unusual for them to kill children."

Helen motioned for Rebekah to lean closer. In an even lower voice she continued. "Rebekah, there is even a more frightening problem." She glanced once more at the door. "There seems to be a big business going on that involves people at very high levels of government and," she hesitated, "the medical community. I don't know much about it, but it seems that selling organs harvested from children is a lucrative business."

Rebekah turned pale. Her mouth went dry and her eyes began to tear. She had never considered that her own profession could be involved in such hideous acts of murder for profit. But something deep within began to cause a very uneasy feeling.

"Oh my God! Helen, are you sure?" Rebekah's voice was almost a whisper.

"I can't be completely sure, but the children on the streets report kids being lured into large, fancy cars with promises of money or drugs and then are never seen again. I am not an investigator, but whenever I have inquired about it here at the office, I have met a stone wall of silence."

The coworker returned and their conversation ended. Rebekah arranged for Helen to take her to visit the street kids the next week.

Rebekah met Helen at nine at night that following Wednesday. Helen carried a small, black backpack. Instead of heading to the busy streets where Rebekah had gone before, Helen walked down several side streets; she seemed to know exactly where she was going. After nearly fifteen minutes, Helen stopped. She pointed to an empty building and said, "I have been coming here for several years. The kids out on the main streets are on edge; they can be pretty aggressive, as you know. They feel vulnerable. The kids back here are more relaxed."

She turned and walked into the dark opening and climbed three flights of stairs. They turned down a dismal hallway. It was covered in empty bottles, trash was strewn everywhere. Rebekah immediately smelled the odor of urine and human waste. She closed her mouth and tried not to breathe too deeply.

About halfway down the hall, Helen called out, "Hello, it's me Helen. I have a friend with me. It's okay."

They stopped and listened. It was perfectly silent except for the neighborhood sounds outside. Rebekah was frightened standing in a darkened hallway in an empty building. She was glad Helen was there.

Helen stood quietly waiting. Then, from the end of the hall came a child's voice. "Helen is that you?"

"Yes, it's me. Everything's fine. You are safe," she replied.

Rebekah could not see any movement, but she heard the sounds of people moving in the dark.

"We're at the end of the hall. Come on in," the voice said.

Helen and Rebekah made their way down the hallway, carefully stepping over dank piles of garbage. They reached the end of the corridor and entered the room on the right. There was dull light peaking in from the street below. It took Rebekah's eyes a few moments to adjust. Slowly she began to see the forms of children sitting around the room on the floor.

"Are you all right?" Helen asked.

There was a pause. "The police and soldiers are out tonight," said one of the faceless voices. "It's not safe when they're patrolling."

Helen and Rebekah joined the children sitting on the floor. Helen introduced Rebekah but didn't tell them she was a doctor. Helen carried on small talk with the kids; they obviously knew her well. Before long they were talking nonstop, giving her a full report of all that had happened since her last visit.

There were five girls and three boys in the group. Rebekah could not see their faces well, so she had no idea of how old they were. By the sound of their voices, she guessed twelve or thirteen. Rebekah noticed cardboard boxes flattened on the floor and a few blankets by one of the children. Garbage was everywhere; empty bottles, cans, newspapers and plastic bags lay randomly on the floor. Rebekah saw something next to her foot. She leaned forward and squinted to see what it was. She could not make out its shape, so reached out and felt the cold steel of the needle of a syringe. She carefully moved it to one side.

Helen pulled her backpack off her shoulders and placed it in front of her. As the children continued to talk, she opened the pack to reveal cans of food, bread, and some candies, two bars of soap and one tube of toothpaste. The children moved closer to the presents. Rebekah felt two of them move close to her. She thought they just wanted to be near Helen's gifts, but noticed they did not move away.

One of the girls took her hand and put both of hers around it, holding on tightly. On the other side, another girl put both her arms through Rebekah's upper arm and laid her head just below her shoulder. Neither girl said a word. At this close distance, Rebekah saw she had been wrong in her estimation of their ages. These two girls could not be more than ten or eleven years old, perhaps younger.

Rebekah looked at Helen. The other kids had gathered around her, several talking at once. Some were stroking her hair; others were holding her hands; some just leaned against her. Her two girls slowly started asking questions. Where was she from? How old was she? Did she have a family? The questions went on and on.

After more than an hour, Helen told the kids they had to be going. None of the children wanted them to leave. Finally Helen stood, kissed each of the dirty faces, and said she would be back. Rebekah felt awkward, but she kissed the children as well and said goodbye. The kids clung on as long as possible and finally released their grip when Rebekah and Helen reached the front entrance. With a final farewell wave, Helen and Rebekah walked down the street, leaving the youngsters standing alone in the night.

Neither Rebekah nor Helen said much on their taxi ride to Helen's flat. Just before they parted, Rebekah looked at her small friend and said, "Helen, thank you for introducing me to your friends. I can tell they love you a lot. It's so curious. Before we went tonight, I was thinking of all the things I could do as a doctor to help them. But it is not programs or money they are desperate for, it's to be loved. To know someone cares. So simple and yet so profound."

Rebekah decided to walk the rest of the way home from Helen's rather than take a bus. There was a small restaurant near her apartment. She took a table near the back. She washed her hands several times in the bathroom but still felt dirty. The waiter took her order, a large salad, and disappeared. The young girl in the emergency room came to mind. It had been purely intuitive for her to cradle the dying girl in her arms and yet that was probably the best thing she could have done. The children tonight ... all they wanted was someone to love them, to hold them, to show them human kindness. She wanted desperately to go directly to Elisabeth and Dr. Aziz, but it was too late. She would have to wait a few more days for their weekly meeting.

Chapter Twenty-Five

Elisabeth opened the door and gave Rebekah her customary hug and kiss. Rebekah knew something of what the street kids needed in the way of human touch and warmth. Every time she was with Elisabeth, her soul felt peaceful, safe, secure. There were times when Rebekah just wanted Elisabeth to hold her.

"Rebekah, how very nice to see you," Dr. Aziz said. He was sitting at his desk, looking over some papers.

Rebekah took her seat on the sofa. Dr. Aziz stood up and walked over to her. He started to say something, then stopped. He rubbed his chin and looked at her over the rim of his glasses.

Rebekah looked up; their eyes met. The kind eyes looked at the troubled eyes. Dr. Aziz went back to his desk and leaned against it, folded his arms. He waited. "Well, what is it, Rebekah?" he asked in his fatherly voice, an easy smile on his face.

"Am I that easy to read?" she asked in a soft tone.

"Let's just say you do not hide your feelings well," Dr. Aziz responded.

"I have something I want you and Elisabeth to give me your counsel on," Rebekah said.

His eyebrows moved higher as if inviting more information. He put his hand out like a policeman does to stop traffic; he walked to the door and spoke to an empty hallway. "Elisabeth, can you come in for a moment? The good doctor would like our advice." He turned and smiled at Rebekah.

Elisabeth appeared in the doorway with a look of concern on her face. "Is everything all right Rebekah?" she asked.

"Yes, Elisabeth, everything is just fine." She hesitated.

The Aziz's knew all of the recent events in detail. She had wept on Elisabeth's shoulder as she recounted the girl in the emergency room.

Dr. Aziz had turned red with anger when she spoke of her first encounter with the street bullies, his father's heart wanting to protect his child.

"Last week, I went back to the streets with a friend," Rebekah said with bowed head.

Elisabeth reached out and put her hand on Rebekah's hand. "Rebekah, that is so dangerous. Are you hurt?" She looked deeply trying to read Rebekah's eyes.

"No, not at all. But I do have something I want to discuss with you. As you know, after the encounter with the dying girl, I had all these plans to set up medical clinics, schools, homes, drug abuse homes, battered children shelters; my mind was going wild with ideas because the need is so great." Rebekah dropped her head slightly, thinking.

She looked up. "I just read four articles about Mother Teresa and her work in India. She established homes where people came to die. There people would not die alone, but with someone holding them. I had no idea at the time, but when that young girl died in my arms, it was a form of ministry."

"My question is this: after what Dr. Asbury said about women in general and me in particular, what am I to do?" She looked full face at Dr. Aziz. Rebekah did not wait for an answer, but continued on. "Do I submit this to Reverend Habib to get his permission? Do I submit this to the board of elders? Do I just do it on my own? I have some money Miss Lovejoy gave me. I could buy a house and start tomorrow. She looked at Dr. Aziz first and then to Elisabeth. "What do I do?"

"My goodness, Rebekah," said Dr. Aziz, "you certainly have a way of hitting on all the major issues at once. Any one of the things you just mentioned could start World War three in our church — and you want to take them on all at once." He was smiling, his eyes bright. "I like a good fight, but we must choose our battles carefully," he said confidently.

"Let me ask you a question, Rebekah. Is it possible to be obedient and in rebellion?" Dr. Aziz glanced at Elisabeth.

"Well, I suppose so," Rebekah said without much enthusiasm. "If you fear the consequences enough, you may not disobey someone but not really be in submission. Maybe it would be like a schoolboy who dislikes his teacher, but because he fears a whipping, does what he is told. Or maybe a better example would be prisoners under a harsh guard. They may obey, because he has a gun and can punish them, but they are not at all submissive."

"Rebekah, let me ask you this. Can you be in submission and yet not obey?" asked Dr. Aziz.

Rebekah looked at Elisabeth to see if she would give any indication if this was a trick question. Elisabeth looked back and tilted her head as if to say, "I don't know either."

Rebekah liked being put on the spot and having to think outside the customary boxes. "Perhaps it could be possible, if someone asked me to do something that was wrong, that I would not obey them. But I would not necessarily be in rebellion, I just wouldn't obey," she said matter-of-factly.

"So obedience and disobedience do not necessarily have anything to do with submission or rebellion. Is that what you are saying?" Dr. Aziz liked pushing Rebekah to think.

"They are two different things. One is an action, what you do. The other is an attitude of the heart, an inner disposition," Rebekah countered.

"I think we can safely say that submission is having a heart desire to want to comply with reasonable requests or expectations of those in authority. Rebellion, on the other hand, is when we set out to defy those in authority in order to further our own ends. They are both inner attitudes or dispositions or states of mind." Dr. Aziz paused and reached for a pad of paper on his desk.

It took a few tries before he found a pen that worked; he began writing on the pad. "This is some pretty good stuff. I had better write it down while it's fresh. I won't remember it in the morning," he said sheepishly.

"So was Jesus in rebellion against the authorities of the day or merely disobedient?" Rebekah asked.

"Rebekah, you do have a way of going for the throat." Dr. Aziz stood up and walked to the window.

"I would say Jesus was in absolute submission to the authorities. He just had a higher authority and another set of goals. He was out to do the Father's will and bring about His kingdom. So this set up a series of conflicts; really, I suppose, it is the conflict of two kingdoms. This is what Peter must have faced when he was commanded to stop preaching. He was pressed: who would he obey, God or man? Paul faced similar circumstances and we are still facing them today." Dr. Aziz's voice sounded a bit weary.

"So, if it's possible to be submissive and disobedient, then what keeps everyone from doing whatever they want, whenever they want? Isn't that a recipe for chaos?" Rebekah questioned. She had never seen Dr. Aziz as uncomfortable as he was now.

"I suppose this brings us back to the greatest and most fundamental principle of the faith: our love for one another. This is not primarily an emotion; it is an act of the will to consistently choose the highest good for God, others, and ourselves. We must also guard our hearts, to make sure no malice or bitterness or hatred is allowed a resting place."

"But how do we do this practically? Dr. Asbury has already forbidden me or any woman to have a role in the church. I am not sure what Reverend Habib thinks. I certainly cannot do this ministry alone. The best people to help would be those who know me, and that would be folks from the church. Don't I need to first get permission from Reverend Habib?"

"I think as a matter of courtesy and information, we should talk to Reverend Habib and hopefully get his blessing. But the bigger question is, what do we do if both Dr. Asbury and Reverend Habib oppose us?" Dr. Aziz asked.

Rebekah noticed that Dr. Aziz had stopped using "you," and was now using us. Did that mean Dr. Aziz wanted to be a part of the ministry?

"I think we should arrange a meeting with Dr. Asbury and Reverend Habib soon. But first I want to finish our talks. Then we can meet and see what happens." He sounded pensive but confident.

Dr. Aziz looked at his watch. "I see it is too late to have our session tonight."

"But, Dr. Aziz, I can't bear the wait! What do I do if Dr. Asbury and Reverend Habib do not allow me to do this ministry?" Rebekah was clearly agitated.

"Then I suppose you must answer the basic question — who will you obey, God or man?"

Chapter Twenty-Six

Dr. Thomas Asbury sat perfectly upright at his large, polished desk. He leaned back in the black leather chair, his hands folded behind his head. He required the cleaning staff to thoroughly go over every square inch of his office each morning before he arrived. A new writing pad had been placed carefully on the right side of his desk, with his favorite pen lying upon it. Thomas would arrive at precisely nine forty-five each morning, lead the staff in a fifteen-minute Bible study, and then enter his office by ten. Within a minute or two of his arrival, Ruth, his secretary, would bring him fresh coffee with a splash of cream and one sugar cube, already stirred. Dr. Thomas Asbury loved order.

His boyish good looks made him appear younger than his thirty-two years. His dress was ultra modern. Twice a year, he would return to the United States for meetings, stopping in London or New York to buy the finest suits. Twice a week, the manicurist would come to his office to clean, round, and polish his nails.

Thomas was pleased with the progress. He had been at his job just over two years and had seen remarkable changes. Once word spread about the meeting with Rebekah, any thought of resisting his rule vanished. The look of fear on the faces of the pastors and elders in that meeting said it all. He knew from that moment on he was in complete control. Thomas thought someone might speak up to defend her, but no one said a word. The victory was a bit disappointing. He had hoped for more of a fight.

The phone rang. He could tell by the tone it was an internal call. He looked at the light to see it was his secretary. He picked up the receiver and spoke, "Yes, Ruth, what is it?"

"Jonathan is here for the eleven o'clock appointment," Ruth said.

"Make him wait five minutes and then send him in." Thomas did not want it appear that access to him was too easy.

Jonathan had only been in the country for four months. Thomas had requested an assistant to do most of the in-country traveling to keep an eye on the outlying churches and programs. Thomas hated the heat, the bad food, the threat of sickness, and the general discomfort of going outside the capital city. Jonathan seemed to be capable enough; he was several years older than Thomas and had spent the previous five years working for the United Nations in Central Asia. His English accent and quiet manners gave him an air of superiority. Thomas liked that.

"Good morning. Dr. Asbury. You wanted to see me?" Jonathan said as he entered the office.

"Good morning to you, Jonathan. Please, why don't we sit out on the veranda. Would you like something to drink?"

"No, sir, I am fine."

Thomas pushed the screen door open that led to the large, vine-covered veranda. The gardens surrounding the headquarters were beautifully kept by a full staff of local workers. It was a pleasant morning. Dr. Asbury examined the chair carefully, making sure there was no dirt to stain his new suit. He was not satisfied and called for one of the workers to come and clean off the chair. Jonathan was already seated.

"Well, how did your trip go?" Thomas asked.

Jonathan had just returned the day before from a visit to twelve churches in the delta area of the country. It was an arduous ten-day journey. Jonathan was still weary. "In general the trip went quite well. My driver would have made a very good kamikaze pilot. My forearms are sore from grabbing on to the dashboard." He said smiling and rubbing his arms.

Thomas saw little value in humor, but said nothing. He looked at Jonathan intently waiting, for his report.

"To be honest, I think we have a problem," Jonathan continued. "The five-year strategic plan you presented at the last conference is not sitting well with the pastors. They felt they had no say in what is being required of them. Consequently, they are resistant, to say the least."

Thomas unconsciously folded his arms across his chest and leaned back in his chair. "Jonathan, you know as well as I do that these people are like children. They have no idea how to run a large enterprise like this denomination. They only see their small local picture and not the big one that I see.

"The pastors that are not willing to change and embrace my vision need to be removed. Most of them are older and will only get in my way. Besides, we can save money by bringing in young pastors fresh out of seminary," Thomas said in an even tone.

"Jonathan, you know darn well it's all about power in the final analysis. I have it and they want it. The only thing I can do is root out those who would challenge me and bring in people who will go along with the plan. I will not have my vision for the future jeopardized by a bunch of ignorant pastors." Although Thomas did not raise his voice, Jonathan felt cold steel in his words.

It took Jonathan nearly two hours to give a full report of his trip. Thomas asked for a written report to be on his desk in two working days. He mentioned specifically that he wanted the names of the pastors Jonathan thought most resistant to his plan for the future.

The meeting with Jonathan put him in a sour mood for the remainder of the afternoon. He looked at his agenda and saw he was attending a working dinner with the wife of the president of the country and several political and business figures that evening. The First Lady was hosting a special dinner to discuss what could be done about the rampant spread of AIDS in the country. Thomas could care less about the AIDS victims; only idiots got AIDS these days. "They should protect themselves, like I do," he thought. He checked his watch; he still had time for a round of golf before the dinner. He called the club and arranged a teetime. His driver picked him up in front of the office building and within the hour he had eaten, changed, and was ready for his favorite pastime. He played poorly which only heightened his already foul mood.

The presidential palace was an impressive building, constructed during the colonial days. As Thomas waited for the driver to pull in front of the main entrance, he noticed several stretch limousines also waiting. Thomas noted that his Mercedes looked small compared to the other beautiful limos ahead of him. A twinge of insecurity shot through him.

Thomas walked into the main dining hall and was immediately greeted by the First Lady's chief of staff. This made him feel somewhat better. People were being ushered to their seats. He was escorted to the far end of the last table, next to the owner of a coat manufacturing plant. He quickly recognized that the people with power were all seated at the table with the First Lady or close by. He felt slighted and anger began to simmer within. Thomas did not listen to one word spoken. He looked at his watch continually and left as soon as he could without causing embarrassment. When he got to the car, the driver was nowhere to be found. He waited for nearly thirty minutes before the surprised driver returned. By then, Thomas was furious.

Simon had been hiding at Dr. Asbury's house for nearly two years. It was a good life for an orphan street kid. Since Robert's murder, Simon was content to merely be alive. He worked in the garden and enjoyed seeing the plants grow and produce beautiful flowers. He liked putting his hands into the soil and feeling the warmth and smelling the rich, fertile ground. But he was also tired of the routine. He felt confined, lonely. He missed his friends and life on the streets. He wanted to leave.

Simon heard Dr. Asbury's car arrive and honk the horn once. The gardener was waiting. He grunted as he lifted the heavy gate and pulled it open just enough to let the car drive past. The gardener grunted again getting the gate closed for the night. A single angry voice broke the silence of Simon's shelter. Dr. Asbury was yelling at the driver. Simon could not hear the words, but he knew the tone. Simon's mouth went dry, his heart raced and his stomach tightened with fear. "Not tonight, please, not tonight." Simon dreaded being with Dr. Asbury when he was angry. He could be very cruel.

The driver tried to apologize, but Thomas ignored him slamming the door to underscore this anger. He stormed into the house. A few minutes later, he came outside, seeking the gardener who was standing near his small shack. No words were exchanged. Thomas signaled and the gardener merely turned to summon Simon.

A few minutes passed and Simon hoped Dr. Asbury had gone to bed. At the door to his tiny hut Simon saw a shadow appear. It was the gardener.

"Dr. Asbury wants you." He turned and walked back to his shack and waited. He kept a careful eye out to make sure Simon went immediately.

Simon followed the stone path past the pool and crossed the grass that led to the outside entrance of Dr. Asbury's bedroom. He knocked lightly on the window. Dr. Asbury opened the door immediately. Simon went in without a word.

Thomas was very upset and took his anger out on Simon. When he was finished, he put on his robe and motioned for Simon to leave. Still naked, Simon sat on the edge of the bed. Robert would have known better, but Simon thought he owed Dr. Asbury an explanation why he wanted to leave. It was a big mistake.

"Dr. Asbury, I appreciate you letting me stay here and giving me a job, but I want to leave and go back to my friends," Simon said evenly.

Thomas had his back to Simon. He did not say anything for a long time. When he did finally turn to face Simon, his face was contorted into an awful scowl. Simon could have sworn his eyes were now a violent yellow-green color, not the normal blue.

"So you want to leave?" Thomas hissed.

"You are under my control and you will leave when I tell you to leave." Thomas was now walking toward Simon.

Thomas scanned the room, eyeing his thick, black, leather belt lying on the chair. He walked over and calmly picked it up making sure the large, gold buckle swung free. Simon was unprepared for the speed Dr. Asbury showed as he flew across the room and hit Simon across the face with the buckle end of the leather weapon. Simon felt the impact before he realized what had happened. Stunned, he fell back on the bed. Before his head hit the sheets he was struck again. Dr. Asbury was now shouting and cursing and beating with a vengeance.

Suddenly the door to the bedroom opened and Dr. Asbury's wife, Kathy, came in.

"Thomas, are you all right? I heard voices and I...." She looked directly at Thomas and saw the belt in his raised hand. She then looked at the bed to see blood splattered sheets and Simon naked, cowering on the bed. She stood frozen, taking in the horrific sight.

Thomas lunged at his wife and grabbed her by the hair. With adrenaline-induced strength, he threw her toward the door. "Get out of here, you stupid bitch!" he screamed. He had meant to throw her into the hallway, but in his rage his aim was off and he threw her into the doorpost. Her head bounced back. She remained standing but could not move. Blood ran down the side of her face from a deep cut on her forehead. "I said get out!" Thomas shouted again and hit her square on the jaw with his fist. Spittle and blood flew out of the side of her mouth, landing on the white wall and ran down together in one small rivulet. Kathy fell hard on the floor, her head in the hallway, her feet still in the bedroom. Thomas was now standing over her. He banged the door against her legs, screaming for her to get out. She crawled out the door and laid in the hallway, her consciousness waning.

He now returned to Simon, with renewed energy, and began to savagely beat him. It lasted for more than twenty minutes. When he was physically exhausted and could beat no more, he drug Simon's body to the outside door and pushed him onto the grass, slamming the door behind him.

"Nobody leaves me," he shouted, alone in the room.

Simon laid on the wet grass until nearly daylight. He slowly regained consciousness and crawled and stumbled back to his shack. He waited several days, trying to gain some strength. Early one morning he put his few possessions in a plastic bag and slowly moved toward the gate. The gardener watched him go. He could easily find another. Simon slipped out the gate and was back on the streets. "Life couldn't possibly get any worse." He thought. He was wrong.

Chapter Twenty-Seven

Elisabeth met Rebekah at the door. "Young lady, I don't care if you are a doctor, when you get sick I want you to come over here and let me look after you.

"I went to your place last week and even though you were ill you kept going," Elisabeth continued. "Just look at you! You look awful." Elisabeth put her mother's hand on Rebekah's cheek to see if there was a fever. "I made you some soup; homemade soup is always the best medicine." Rebekah bent down and kissed Elisabeth's wrinkled forehead and put her arm around her shoulder.

"I am fine now, Elisabeth. And I promise next time to check myself into your personal clinic." Rebekah greeted Dr. Aziz warmly and he too inquired how she was feeling. It felt good knowing someone cared.

Without much fanfare, Dr. Aziz launched straight into the subject at hand. "We have a lot of ground to cover this evening," he said.

"I want to first talk about the issue of what is sometimes called headship. Other related issues are those of submission and obedience, which we have discussed. But let's start by reading First Corinthians. Let's start in chapter eleven and look at the first of the problem passages. Why don't you read it, Rebekah?"

Rebekah reached down on the floor and picked up her large handbag. After a minute or two of rummaging, she found it hiding at the bottom.

She found the passage and began to read, "'I praise you for remembering me in everything and for holding to the teachings just as I passed them on to you. Now I want you to realize that the head of every man is Christ and the head of the woman is man, and the head of Christ is God.'" She stopped, but Dr. Aziz asked her to read on. When she finished chapter fourteen, Dr. Aziz said that was enough for now.

"What is the context of verse three, Rebekah?" he asked.

"Paul seems to be addressing how public worship was to be done and what is appropriate for a woman to wear on her head. I just noticed that Paul, in talking about praying or prophesying, does not make an issue about women doing it, but how they do it. That's interesting."

"We will come back to that point when we discuss the issue of women being quiet in church; but for now, just make a mental note that women praying and prophesying in church was the norm not the exception and that Paul goes on to bring correction to men and women alike.

"But for now the verse we must understand is verse three. What does it mean?"

"The key word seems to be head," Rebekah said. "What does the word mean?"

"What does it mean in English?" asked Dr. Aziz.

Rebekah replied. "Well, the first thing that comes into my mind is the physical head. But we also use the word to mean someone in charge of something, like the head of a department or a government. Is that what this means?"

"That is the question. And right off we do not have agreement, even among scholars. The Greek word that Paul uses is "kephale." And, as in English, it can mean the physical head.

"However, this is where scholars do not agree. Some argue that the primary meaning is one who has authority or leadership over something or someone. But there is no agreement. There are many scholars who believe the primary meaning is source or origin.

"When we talk about the headwaters of a river, we mean the source or origin. I did some further research and found that one of my dictionaries listed forty-eight English meanings of the Greek word "kephale" and not one of them meant leader, authority, first, or supreme. On the other hand, in one of my other lexicons, there was one reference to 'superior rank' as a definition."

"So what do you do?" Rebekah leaned closer.

"Remember Rebekah, I told you this is not a science. The only honest answer is that we don't know precisely what Paul meant."

"Well that's a big help," Rebekah said. She gave Dr. Aziz a smug look; the look scientists, those who know, give to philosophers, those who guess.

Dr. Aziz had seen the look before; he acknowledged her smugness and continued. "In light of what we have learned about Paul and women, his inclusion, his recognition of their leadership and service in the church, and as you pointed out Paul's non-issue with them praying and prophesying in church, what do you think he meant?"

"I know which one I would like for it to be, but that doesn't make it the correct one," Rebekah replied quickly.

"This is where we must dig deeper. I looked up some information from the Septuagint, which is basically the Old Testament translated into Greek. Paul most likely made reference to it in his studies. Where the Hebrew word for head — the body part — was used, the Greek word used was translated 'kephale' ninety-five percent of the time. However, when the Hebrew word clearly meant ruler or leader, the translators only used 'kephale' five percent of the time. The other ninety-five percent they used another Greek word. This gives us the indication that the Greek word 'kephale,' that Paul uses in this passage, most likely did not mean leader or ruler."

"Let's do an experiment. See I can talk science too," Dr. Aziz said happily. "Replace the word 'head' in the passage with 'ruler' and 'leader' and see if it makes sense. Then let's do the same thing, but use the words 'source' or 'origin.' And in light of the entire New Testament, let's see which best fits the overall theme. Read the passage again and replace the terms, please Rebekah."

Rebekah began, "Now I want you to realize that the ruler/leader of every man is Christ, and the ruler/leader of a woman is man, and the ruler/leader of Christ is God."

"Is this statement true or not, Rebekah?"

"No, it's not. First of all, Jesus is not the leader of every person. There are many millions who have chosen not to follow or acknowledge his leadership. Look at all the evil in the world; certainly this is not the result of Jesus leading these people. I suppose, in a very general sense, one could say that Jesus is the ruler of the universe, but I don't think that was what Paul was saying. I am not sure about the next phrase. I am not sure what woman he is referring to. Is that correct that it is singular, a woman? If it is, then who is the man? That is not clear at all."

"That's fine, Rebekah, we will come back to that in a minute, but yes you are correct. Paul switches from the universal to the particular, or singular in this phrase and then back again. What about the last phrase?"

"That seems to be filled with problems as well. I do not know much about the Trinity, but I have always assumed they were equals. This makes it sound like God is the ruler and leader and Jesus is the follower or subject. Would God refer to God the Father or God the Holy Spirit? Does that mean that Jesus is lesser than the others? That creates a much bigger dilemma than women's role in the church. It would undermine the whole concept of the Godhead, and that sounds much more serious."

"Trust me Rebekah, in the environment Paul was writing, he would never insinuate that Jesus and God were not equals. Paul was arguing this exact issue with the Greeks. They were trying to say that Jesus was not God at all, but simply a ghost-like creature, an emanation of God and not truly God or man.

"So Paul would never give them more ammunition. But let's go back to the second phrase. You noted that Paul had switched to the singular. Actually it should read '... the ruler/leader of a woman is the man.' Taken literally, this is very problematic indeed. Is Paul saying that any man has authority over any woman, Christian or not?

"Is he saying that any man in the church has authority or leadership over any other women? Then what about the wives of other men? Does a son rule over his mother at any age? This cannot possibly be what Paul meant.

"Let's look at the other possibility. Read it again, Rebekah, but use source/origin instead of head."

Rebekah crossed her legs and leaned forward putting her Bible on her lap. She began to read, "'Now I want you realize that the source/origin of every man is Christ, the source/origin of a woman is the man, and the source/origin of Christ is God.' This makes so much sense! Of course Jesus is the source of creation. Woman was made from man, so in a sense, he was her source. And God, in this context could be said to be the source of sending Jesus into the world. This is really amazing!"

"WHAT is so amazing?" Elisabeth said as she walked through the door, the usual tray in hand.

Rebekah immediately tried explaining what she and Dr. Aziz had just been talking about. She did a very good job and with only a few prompts from Dr. Aziz, she gave Elisabeth a clear summary. Rebekah continued excitedly to explain the concept to Elisabeth.

"Excuse me, ladies, but we still have much more work to do. While Rebekah is drinking her tea, Elisabeth, will you be kind enough to read Ephesians, chapter five? We need to look at the issue of submission and obedience. To get the overall idea, please start at verse one and read to the end of the chapter. Actually, read to the end of chapter six."

When Elisabeth finished, Dr. Aziz began speaking.

"This is the best indication that Paul had no idea that people would be pouring over every word and sentence he dictated. If he'd had any idea his writings would be thoroughly scrutinized for the next two thousand years he would surely have cleaned up his sentence structure and grammar. Verses fifteen through twenty-three form one very long and complicated sentence.

"To make verse twenty-two a separate sentence is a travesty. To further separate the thought by placing it into a separate paragraph, like most modern translations do, is simply incorrect, in my opinion."

"But isn't it clear in the Greek where one sentence starts and the other ends?" Rebekah set her teacup down as she asked the question.

"Not exactly. As I mentioned, we have no originals. The material scribes copied on was expensive so they tried to get as much information as they could on each sheet of the papyrus.

"The scribes would use, at least early on, all upper case letters and simply run them together, leaving out punctuation marks and spaces. In many cases, it is very difficult, if not impossible, to know the original structure. And of course, Paul did not sit down and write these himself; he would most likely be pacing back and forth dictating them aloud as a scribe wrote down his words. When you are speaking, it is much easier to ramble than when you are writing."

Rebekah and Elisabeth looked at each other and nodded their heads in agreement. "Present company excluded, of course," Dr. Aziz said without missing a beat.

"To understand what Paul is trying to say then, we must go back to the beginning of the sentence. The imperative statement comes in verse eighteen, when Paul commands them to be filled with the Spirit. He then goes on to define what that will look like: speaking, singing, making music, always giving thanks, and submitting to one another.

"So one of the characteristics of being filled with the Spirit is mutual submission. This is nothing short of revolutionary. Remember Rebekah, we have seen what the Greek, Roman, and Jewish concepts of women were. To now require that the husband submit to the wife, to love her and hold her in esteem, was completely new. Paul was saying that, in the Kingdom of God, human relationships would be different than those of the world.

"The relationship between man and fellow man, man and woman, parents and children, the fellowship of believers — in every way, relationships were to take on a drastically different set of values. In the post-redemptive Kingdom of God, we were all equal. So rather than Paul putting women down, he was elevating them to equality with men — the exact opposite of the world's way. But you come to expect that with God. After all, the ruler of this worldly kingdom is the opposite of God in every way. So their kingdoms are completely different as well.

"Some want to use verse thirty-three as a way to suppress women, by saying that no matter what the husband does, the wife is to respect him. But when you look at the Greek, this is not an imperative statement to the wife. The verb 'to respect' is clearly in the subjunctive. It means that Paul is expressing a desire, a hope, a wish, not a command.

"Also, this clause is introduced by the Greek word which means 'in order that.' So what Paul says is: 'husbands love your wives in such a way that they would have the desire to show you the husband, respect.'

"Something of great interest in this passage is what Paul did NOT say. He never instructs the wife to obey. Now, Elisabeth, don't get any ideas." Dr. Aziz reached over and put his hand on hers. He gave her a big smile and continued.

"In the time and culture in which Paul was writing, this was earth shaking. He goes on to tell slaves to obey and children to obey, but not wives. Paul is truly turning the world upside down. This first and foremost elevates the woman to the same status as the man.

"In Galatians, this same Paul says one of the most liberating and controversial statements of the day: 'there is neither Jew nor Greek, male nor female, slave nor free, for you are all one in Christ Jesus.' Are the wives to be submissive and obedient to their husbands? Yes, of course. But are the husbands to submit and obey their wives? Yes, of course. What Paul is stating is a new way of living that reflects the new freedom we have in Christ. It is not gender dominated, but motivated and guided by mutual love and mutual respect. Don't you think this is the better way?"

"All I can say is you are going to get yourself in a lot of trouble if you start teaching this to your students or speaking about it in church," Rebekah noted.

"That is probably true Rebekah, so if I am going to be a martyr, I had better make sure to get all the issues on the table, so it will be worth it," Dr. Aziz said with a bright look in his eyes.

"That having been said, let's move on to another controversial passage. Rebekah, you have already read First Corinthians fourteen, but please read verses twenty-six through forty again."

Rebekah finished reading the passage and looked at Dr. Aziz.

"What stands out to you? Don't try to analyze it yet; just tell me what you notice."

"Without giving it much thought, the thing that caught my attention was again how inclusive Paul seemed to be. He used the words everyone, all, each one. I also noticed that he said, on three occasions, that certain individuals should keep silent. Let me see if I can find them. Oh, here they are. Verses twenty-eight and thirty, and of course thirty-four — the one about women."

"And what was the context?" Dr. Aziz asked.

"The little heading in my Bible, just before this passage says, 'Orderly Worship.' So, I suppose it is in the context of how to conduct an orderly worship service."

"What can you assume from this text?"

"That the church in Corinth was having problems with order in their services. Sounds like it was pretty chaotic."

"Right. Rebekah, now let me try and give some background. The church in Corinth was most certainly made up of a mixture of cultures. Greeks and Jews probably dominated, but given the location and economic power of the city, every ethnic group of the Mediterranean was represented. It was a melting pot of pagan cultures.

"Corinth had a terrible reputation for both opulence and debauchery. There was actually a word in Greek, 'korinthiazstai,' which meant to live like a Corinthian — which meant in immorality and drunkenness. While the upright women of Greece were secluded, the temple prostitutes and other loose women were free to ply their trade. It was noted that one temple had more than one thousand prostitutes.

"Pagan festivals and celebrations were often characterized by wild music, frenzied dancing, drunkenness, and sexual orgies. Riotous chaos would reign supreme for days at a time. This was the normal way to celebrate and worship the pagan gods. You can imagine the impact when these folks started coming to Christ from this lifestyle and entered the church to celebrate and worship.

"Paul only spent eighteen months there, so he could not have had much time to deeply instill what was expected, especially if new converts kept joining the church after Paul left, which they most certainly did. The letters of First and Second Corinthians are part of an ongoing dialogue over a period of five or six years. This dialogue was by letters sent back and forth and by delegations coming to Ephesus to query Paul directly.

"So that sets up the situation in chapter fourteen. Your observations were correct. Paul was trying to do a balancing act; he wanted all, everyone, each one to participate but not in a disorderly way. So Paul is simply saying, 'Do not all try to speak at once, as you might have done at your pagan celebrations but worship peacefully. While one is speaking, the others should be quiet. Tell me, Rebekah, why is it important to be silent?'

"If everyone is making noise, you can't hear very well. Also, if everyone is talking, it is difficult to learn."

"That's it. We often use the phrase 'be quiet.' At least I do in my classrooms, when I want to teach. You can certainly learn more with your mouth closed. So part of what Paul is saying has to do with building up the church by being orderly.

"However that is not the explanation for verses thirty-four and thirty-five. Here again, we have a conflict among scholars. As I mentioned before, it is difficult in some passages to know how to punctuate. And how we punctuate has a great deal to do with meaning. In this case, one little period makes a big difference.

"If we place the period after ... 'as in all the churches of the saints,' then begin a new paragraph with 'Let the women keep silent ...' it separates the next phrase from the universal statement that Paul just made. On the other hand, if we place the period midway through verse thirty-three, just after...'for God is not a God of disorder but of peace,' then go to a new paragraph, starting with 'As in all the congregations...women should be silent ...' it means something very different.

"In this case, the phrase about women being silent is attached to the universal statement Paul makes about all the churches. This would mean that, in all the churches Paul requires the women to be silent. This contradicts what Paul said from chapter eleven onwards, so this cannot possibly be the meaning.

"For many years scholars have argued about the position of verses thirty-four and thirty-five. Many ancient manuscripts have these two verses in a different place all together, after verse forty. There is strong evidence that verses thirty-four and thirty five are a quote from the letter sent to Paul from the church in Corinth.

"As I mentioned, ancient Greek punctuation is much different from English. Greek had no quotation marks. The translators have added all the quotation marks in modern translations. But there is a hint that this passage was a quote from the church in Corinth." Dr. Aziz took a yellow pen from the plastic holder inserted in the left-hand pocket of his shirt and wrote on the top of one of his paper pads. He turned it around and showed it to Rebekah and Elisabeth.

"It looks like the letter 'n' with one long leg and a couple of little squiggly lines above it," Elisabeth noted as she looked at Rebekah to see her response.

Rebekah looked at what Dr. Aziz had written and shrugged her shoulders, raised one eyebrow, and nodded.

Dr. Aziz continued. "Paul used this one letter symbol no less than forty-nine times in First Corinthians alone. It has many uses. Sometimes it was used to note the previous passage was a quote. Another usage was as an exclamation showing emotional rebuttal to what had just been said. In English today, we would say, 'What?' 'Nonsense!' or 'No way!' to try and describe the meaning. Technically it is known as an expletive of disassociation. We will see how Paul used it for that purpose in just a minute.

"But first, let's continue with the idea that verses thirty-four and thirty-five were a quote from the Corinthians' letter. At the end of that sentence is this Greek symbol," Dr. Aziz held up his pad and pointed, "Possibly indicating the previous passage was a quote. This would explain why these two verses seem to contradict everything Paul had been saying up until then. Also, in this quote is a reference to the Law referring to the Old Testament. There is no law recorded anywhere in the Old Testament stating that women should be silent. Paul most certainly would not have made such a mistake.

"It was the Jewish legalists in the Corinthian church that were using the added Jewish teaching, from the Mishnah and Talmud – not Old Testament – to once again suppress women. This was not God's law but man's that Paul was fighting against.

"If we go on and look at verses thirty-six and thirty-seven, they make absolutely no sense at all if Paul has just been trying to prove a point about women being silenced in the church. Why? Because Paul then uses the Greek word, the expletive of disassociation, two more times in the following sentences. I can see Paul pacing back and forth dictating his letter to Timothy. In one hand he has the letter from the church in Corinth. They are bragging about how they have silenced the women. Paul is outraged at the Corinthian's arrogance. Another way of saying verses thirty-six and thirty-seven would be, 'Nonsense! Did the word of God originate with you? Are you crazy? Thinking you are the only people it, the truth about women, has reached?'" Dr. Aziz's voice was now at a crescendo, he was nearly shouting at his audience of two. With his hand still raised making the point, he paused, realizing his excess. Slowly he lowered his hand and put it in his worn jacket pocket. It was silent, the kind of silence when truth breaks free from the restraints of ignorance and demands its rightful place.

"This sounds too good," Rebekah said softly. "Are you sure you're not just making this up?" As soon as the words left her mouth, Rebekah realized what she had just done. "Oh, I did not mean it that way. I am not questioning your integrity as a scholar. I mean. Oh, Elisabeth help me!" Rebekah turned toward Elisabeth and playfully buried her head in the cushion on her lap.

Elisabeth reached out to Rebekah and pulled her close. Rebekah felt the kind and gentle hand softly and lovingly stroking her hair. She sat like a child in the arms of a mother soaking in the love. She could hear Dr. Aziz get up and walk to the other side of the room. She looked up sheepishly; he held a magazine in his hand.

"Just to show you I am not a theological fraud," he said with a large smile on his face, "I have here a copy of a respected Christian magazine from the U.S., Christianity Today. In an excellent article, theologian Dr.

Kenneth Kantzer states, 'In First Corinthians fourteen we are caught in an intricate interplay between quotations from a missing letter from the Corinthians and Paul's solutions to problems the letter had raised. The verse is clearly not repeating a law of Scripture and cannot be taken as a universal command for women to be silent in the church. That interpretation would flatly contradict what the apostle had just said three chapters earlier.'

"So, if you cannot believe me, my dear, maybe you can believe Dr. Kantzer and many others." He turned on his heels and placed the magazine on his desk, still chuckling.

Rebekah sat up. "Okay, okay. I'm sorry for questioning your integrity," she said with a touch of sarcasm.

"But if that is the case, what irony! The church has for the past two thousand years used the very argument put forth by Paul's opponents, not Paul, to keep women silent in the church. So the church has used the opposite of what Paul was trying to say in order to continue the subjugation of women. How can they be so far off?" she scoffed.

"Prejudice and ignorance and bigotry die slowly, especially when it is fueled by the ultimate hater of women, Satan, the enemy of all our souls. That is why truth is our only weapon and if we can proclaim it boldly in a spirit of love, truth surely will prevail. But make no mistake Rebekah, many will fight against change and will most certainly resist. That is why it is important to know not only what you believe, but why you believe it. It enables you to stand strong when the storms hit."

Chapter Twenty-Eight

The next weeks were the happiest Rebekah could remember. Her heart felt light and free. "This must be what Jesus was talking about when he said the truth would set us free," she thought. "The thousand pound weight I have been carrying is finally lifted from my shoulders."

On her next visit, Dr. Aziz seemed in a rush to get on with the subject at hand. She had barely seated herself, moving the cushion that she and Elisabeth seemed to share to one side, when Dr. Aziz began speaking.

"We have one last passage we need to look at. Not that these are the only difficult parts of Scripture, there are many. In a way, this is my job security. People will always have questions. Let's look at the passage that is often quoted from First Timothy. Will you be kind enough to read the passage, Rebekah?"

Rebekah had already retrieved her Bible from her bag and had it open. "Would you like me to start at the beginning?"

"As always, that is where one should start to get the full context. Please begin with chapter two and read through chapter three."

Dr. Aziz enjoyed hearing Rebekah's voice. She had a melodious, soothing way of reading the words. Rebekah was obviously a very sophisticated young lady and a fine doctor, but at times Dr. Aziz could hear the little girl still within Rebekah as she read — a slight hint of insecurity, a quick glance to see if her teacher was pleased. He felt sad to think of the suffering, the abandonment, the shame she had experienced, but felt satisfaction that he and Elisabeth were able to help Rebekah move forward with her life.

Listening to her read reminded him of when he helped his own daughters with their schoolwork. They would look up at him with beautiful eyes of wonder and hope, as if to say, "Am I getting it right, papa?"

And he would always reassure them. "Yes, my dear, you're doing just fine." Having Rebekah around was a wonderful joy; she was so eager to learn, so quick to question and challenge, so perceptive to see implications. But he recognized that her greatest quality was her honesty, her openness.

Sometimes her honesty resulted in laughter, but more often they all were left with tears running down their faces as she shared her hurts, her fears, her anger and frustrations. "Oh, how I miss my little girls!" Dr. Aziz pined inwardly.

When Rebekah had finished reading, she looked up.

"The question is always the same. What was Paul saying to Timothy in this passage?"

"It looks as though Paul was instructing him about the attitudes and behavior of the Christians. At first, I thought it was like Corinthians and church order, but I don't see any mention of this being about church order. It is mostly about how Christians should behave." She paused. Dr. Aziz looked up from his Bible and recognized the look.

"Go on, my dear; say it." He was obviously going to be pleased no matter what she said.

"This part about women being saved through childbirth; what in the world does having babies have to do with salvation? Does that mean just because some lady can have multiple births her chances increase for heaven? And does that refer to any woman or just Christians? I don't know Dr. Aziz. That just about goes beyond the boundaries of reason. What does Paul know about having babies anyway?"

"My Rebekah," Elisabeth said as she entered the room, "it is so early in the evening and already you are boiling over. Maybe I should fix you an iced drink to cool you down," she said with a smile.

"Rebekah has actually pinpointed a very interesting topic. You enjoy your tea while I try and paint a picture of the situation Paul was addressing. As we discussed earlier, the city of Corinth was a raucous, wild city of sin and corruption. You could compare it to any modern gambling city where loose living and immorality abound.

"The city of Ephesus was quite different. It was truly one of the grandest cities of ancient times. It sat on the eastern coast of what is today Turkey. Through writings of the day and recent excavations, we are beginning to get a clear picture of how magnificent this city really was.

"As one came into the port, there was a magnificent road that led to the center of town. It was seventy feet wide and paved with marble slabs. Huge columns, more than fifty feet high, lined this great boulevard as far as the eye could see. As one looked up, on the hill above the city stood one of the great wonders of the ancient world: the temple of Artemis. It took more than one hundred and twenty years to build. A huge golden image of Artemis dominated the temple, which also had more than one hundred columns each soaring five stories into the air.

"Artemis was the goddess of fertility, so unspeakable debauchery was commonplace. Ephesus being a major port city for the Roman world was very cosmopolitan. It was also the economic capital for Asia Minor. There were many schools of philosophy, medicine, and the arts, so this was a very sophisticated center of learning. Ephesus, at the time of Paul, is estimated to have been around three hundred thousand people. They had an amphitheatre that would seat more than twenty-five thousand. So this was a very important Roman city.

"Paul went there in about 52 AD on his second missionary journey. He worked closely with his friends Priscilla and Aquila. Together they founded the church in Ephesus. He came back at a later date, most likely around 54 AD, and stayed for two years. We read in Acts that there was a great uproar in the city, because the church was growing rapidly and interfering not only with the religious worship of Artemis but also with the economics of the merchants.

"In any case, Paul left Ephesus and continued his third missionary journey. It is difficult to know from where Paul wrote to Timothy, but we can guess that it was written somewhere close to 62 AD. Much of it depends upon when Paul was executed and scholars do not agree on an exact date. The point is the church in Ephesus was around ten years old. Young Timothy was supposed to be the pastor, but he faced many problems.

"Apparently, Timothy was a quiet and non-assertive individual, given to fear and timidity. Paul had to encourage him to overcome these tendencies in order to fulfill his calling. Timothy had not been well received by the church in Corinth and did not have much success there. So Paul was giving him another chance in Ephesus. Priscilla and Aquila had moved on, most likely back to Rome. Timothy is now on his own, not sure how to lead.

"As in any fertility religion, the priestesses are very influential. In the case of Artemis, the women leaders were very powerful and may have been espousing the idea of the superiority of women over men and the mixing of spiritual ideologies with sexual practices. These priestess' were using sex and religion to dominate and control men.

"Once again, we have a situation where Greek philosophy, mixed with pagan religion and Jewish legalism, caused problems in the church. Pagan ideas were brought into the church through continued conversions of the pagan worshipers. Timothy did not have the strength of personality to correct these influences on his own. Paul heard about the problems in the church and sent Timothy a letter telling him what he should do.

"Throughout the letter, Paul switched back and forth between personal remarks to Timothy and comments about the situation in the church. It is important to note them; perhaps you can do it later.

"For now, let's look at chapter two. To understand this passage, we must clarify what the Greek is saying. In the first seven verses, Paul exclusively uses the Greek word 'anthropos' when referring to man in the universal sense. This word in the Greek is gender inclusive. It simply makes no reference to gender at all, it can also be translated as 'person,' 'humanity,' or 'everyone,' as Paul used it in verse two."

"How do you know that?" Rebekah interrupted. Is it one of the judgment calls or guesses you theologians have to make or can you be certain?" Rebekah asked.

"In this case, there is no question. In Greek, there is an entirely different word for the singular or specific man. The word is 'aner.' One of the most important points in all of Timothy is missed if we are not careful. In verse four, Paul says that God desires all men to be saved; he uses the word 'anthropos' not 'aner.' So Paul is making it a specific point to say God wants everyone, all human beings, men and women to be saved. This completely contradicts the Greek, Roman, and Jewish teachings of selected individuals being picked by God for salvation.

"If Paul had wanted to exclude women and place them forever in subservience, he could have used the word 'aner' and that would have settled the issue once and for all. But no, Paul clearly is saying men and women are equally important before God. Christ died to save everyone. That was God's plan for all of humanity.

"Let's move on. Paul then switches in verse eight. He is talking to particular men, the males of the church in Ephesus. He encourages them to 'lift up holy hands without anger or disputing.' What can you tell from this statement?"

"The men of the church must have been fighting or arguing about something," Rebekah quickly responded.

"Exactly right. Paul is bringing correction to the men in the church. Actually from chapter two verse one to chapter four verse five, Paul is addressing these comments to church order.

"Next, Paul speaks to the women in verse nine. He said, 'in the same way.' Now, some new translations use the word also, but that does not give the proper meaning to what Paul is trying to say. What is the main point here, Rebekah?" Dr. Aziz asked abruptly.

"I have never been any good at sentence structure and diagramming, but I would guess Paul's main point is prayer. And second, perhaps that their hearts stay right, so there would be no fighting and arguing."

"Correct again. Paul is clearly talking about prayer primarily. Actually, one of the early church fathers and commentators on Scripture, St. Chysostom, added 'to pray' to the verse. So it could read 'In the same way I want women to pray, dressed in a becoming manner ...' So once again Paul is certainly not restricting women from participating in the service.

"This next part is important. Paul once again changes his focus. He was speaking about women in general to adorn themselves appropriately. He then changed the tense to address a specific woman. Paul said that this woman, the one causing the problems in the church, should be quiet, in submission, not allowed to teach, and not allowed to have any authority over men in the church.

"It is clear that Paul is addressing this to Timothy. He is saying, 'Timothy, do not give up your God-given place of authority but stand firmly in your position. Do not allow THIS woman to teach false doctrines, SHE must be silent and SHE must not have authority over the men SHE is leading astray.' Paul is in no way offering a general proclamation about women in the church. He is speaking about a particular woman who must have been trying to take over the leadership from Timothy.

"So Paul is saying, 'Stand up to this woman and do no let her control the church, she is bringing in wrong doctrine and confusing the saints, you must stop this woman.' Another clue lies in the word Paul uses when he says 'to have authority over.' It is not the usual word Paul has used many times before, which would have been 'exousia.' Instead, Paul uses the word 'authentien.'

"This is significant because this is the only time in the entire New Testament the word is used. It is a much stronger word, meaning to dominate, to take control, to usurp authority from the legitimate person. Of course, Paul spoke out against such a person; not because she was a woman, but because her behavior was wrong and was endangering the church."

Rebekah and Elisabeth sat quietly for a long time. "What about the comparison Paul makes between Eve and this woman?" Elisabeth asked.

"You still didn't explain about how women having babies is going to save them," Rebekah added.

Dr. Aziz stood perfectly still in front of his two prized pupils, his arms held out to the side. "What do I need to do to get some affirmation? I haven't even had my cup of tea and already I am being verbally assaulted," chuckled Dr. Aziz. "Is there one more cup of tea in the pot, Elisabeth?" Elizabeth poured her husband some tea.

"You two give a man no rest." Dr. Aziz said as he sipped his tea. "Now where were we? Before I answer your questions, let me make one quick observation, lest I forget. In verse eleven, Paul makes another very powerful statement that does not come across clearly in the English.

"Most translations I have looked at use the word 'let' or 'I desire.' This simply does not do justice to the Greek word Paul uses. It is the imperative, a command directed to Timothy to teach her. A better understanding would be to use the word, must. 'This woman must be taught ...'

"This has several implications, the most obvious being that women should be taught the truth. Given their cultural setting, where no women could openly receive an education, Paul commands Timothy to give this woman, the woman causing the trouble, correct teaching.

"The second is not so obvious, but is very telling. It is possible Paul personally knew the woman being referred to, though he never named her. Paul had no hesitation naming Hymenaeus and Alexander at the end of chapter one, but he never names this woman. Some have speculated the reason Paul kept her identity hidden was because he wanted to restore her to fellowship and even leadership in the church. That would be like Paul, who saw himself as a father and mentor to this church.

"Okay, now about the comparison Paul makes between this woman and Eve. The answer is we don't know for sure. Here, we are clearly making a best guess. Most likely the false teaching that was causing the problems in the church may have had something to do with the so-called mystery religions that were commonplace in Ephesus.

"Paul's greatest enemies during his entire ministry were the Greek Gnostics and the Jewish Judaizers. One wanted to pull the early church into the arms of Greek thought and the other wanted to drag the church back into the world of Jewish law.

"The Gnostics were mixing Christianity with the pagan culture and reinterpreting stories from the Old Testament through their pagan world-view. For example, one of the common stories the Gnostics told was that the serpent was good. Eve had become enlightened by listening to him and therefore was the illuminator of the world.

"Later, according to the Gnostic fable, Eve became the mother of Adam, not his wife, and the source of all mankind. So women were supreme. This, of course, fed very nicely into the worship of the goddess Artemis.

"Paul may have directly addressed this issue later in Timothy when he said 'avoid worldly fables ...' Pay attention to 'deceitful spirits and doctrines of demons.' Actually, all the way through Paul's letters to Timothy, he warns him to watch out for these false teachers.

"So in this passage, Paul is simply reminding Timothy of the truth of the Christian teaching. Let's do this phrase by phrase. Paul says in verse thirteen, 'It was Adam who was first created.' He is putting to death the idea that Eve was created first and was the 'goddess Mother' of Adam and all of life.

"Next Paul states, 'It was not Adam who was deceived.' Some Gnostic fables said that Adam was the evil one because he did not want to be enlightened by the serpent. Paul simply says that is not the case. And finally Paul repeats the truth 'But woman being quite deceived, fell into transgression.' Paul was making it very clear that Eve was not enlightened, but made a sinful choice just as Adam did.

"Eve was deceived and Adam sinned with his eyes wide open. Is deception a worse sin than rebellion? Here we must be very careful not to put words or ideas into Paul's statement.

"The early church slipped into the arms of Greek, Roman, and

Jewish thinking regarding women. Many of the early church fathers were influenced by pagan thinking. The result was that women were once again blamed for all the evil, all the temptations, and all the deception. The sad part is that the beauty that God created in woman was villainized — not by the world, but by the church.

"By the fourth century, St. Augustine taught that women were in fact not made in the image of God and could only please the Lord by denying sex and marriage altogether. By the time of Thomas Aquinas in the thirteenth century, Greek philosophy reigned supreme in the church. He taught that women were defective and misbegotten. That is almost a direct quote from our friend Aristotle. And, unfortunately, not much has changed in the last eight hundred years."

The room was quiet. Elisabeth looked at her hands folded on her lap, Rebekah sat forward, elbows on her knees, her chin resting on her hands. Dr. Aziz was standing in front of them thinking but not talking.

"Isn't it interesting?" Rebekah said, breaking the silence. "Whenever we finish talking about the distorted view of women, there is a sense of gloom and depression. But whenever we talk about God's love for women, Jesus' strong stance against the hypocrisy of the Pharisees, or Paul's inclusion and promotion of women, then hope and faith seem to fill the room."

"It is so very true, Rebekah," added Elisabeth. "Whenever we hear man's view of women, it brings a sense of despair; when we speak of God's desires and plans, there is such wonderful hope and expectation."

"That is the nature of truth," Dr. Aziz said as he walked to the window. "It always sets us free. I think it is a very good way to know if we are genuinely on God's path of truth to simply ask the question, 'Is this liberating and setting me free to do God's will and to love Him supremely or is it imposing bonds and burdens on folks that press them down?'"

"May I remind the good professor that there is still one question unanswered?" Rebekah teased cheerfully.

"I have not forgotten, my dear. Let me refill my tea cup and we will continue." Dr. Aziz walked slowly back to his desk and sat on the edge. "Just a reminder, we are still in the singular 'she,' not the universal. I believe it is verse fifteen. Please read it, Rebekah."

"'But women will be saved through childbearing — if they continue in faith, love, and holiness with propriety.' This version says women, not she. How do you explain that?"

"I checked, and of the seven versions, five have 'she' and two have 'women.' The ones that have women will be footnoted at the bottom, showing the Greek says she. It is my opinion the versions that use women are trying to harmonize the sentence.

"They do not pick up one other clear point. The word 'the' is a definite article in front of the word for bearing children. This is a most unusual use of the word as a noun not a verb. By having this word modified by the definite article it should read, 'she will be saved by the childbirth.' Let me make it very clear that there is no unity among the scholarly community about what Paul is trying to say, but I believe I am on as solid ground as anyone.

"Look back at who Paul had just used as an example, Eve. After the fall of man and woman, God explained the consequences to Adam and Eve, but God also planted the seed for redemption by saying that through childbearing the promised redeemer will come. Paul is not referring to just any act of giving birth, but one specific birth that would result in true salvation. Again, Rebekah, what is the point of this sentence?"

"Paul seems to be talking more about salvation than childbearing."

"Indeed, the point here is salvation, not giving birth. How is salvation offered to all fallen man? In all of history there has only been one birth that has brought salvation to the world, the birth of Jesus. Who needs this salvation and redemption? This woman who was in deception, just as Eve was in deception.

"Now in mid-sentence, Paul switches back to the plural, they, 'if they continue in faith, love, and holiness ...' All women in the universe can be saved if they have faith in Jesus, love God, and live holy lives, not simply by having babies."

"Dr. Aziz, this is all so wonderful, but do you mind if I ask a question? If this is true, and I believe that it is, why is it known to so few people? Why don't we hear this more often? It seems to me that all we ever hear is simplistic answers and partial truths, but never go any deeper. We read Bible passages, but for some reason we are afraid to ask the hard questions. Why is that?"

"In a way, the reverence some people have for Scripture can be a blessing, but it can also hinder. For many hundreds of years the churches kept the Scripture out of the hands of ordinary people.

"From their side, they would argue because so many people were uneducated, Scripture was to be entrusted only into the hands of those who could read and interpret it correctly. They wanted to keep heresy out. So the more they emphasized the sacredness of Scripture, the more the people feared doing anything that would tarnish its reputation. The church took the same approach and it became infallible, untouchable, and beyond criticism. But also corrupt.

"It must always be understood that God's word for us must be living and dynamic. If we fear questioning and looking at what it really says, we lose the true essence of its value. But to answer your question as to why, if indeed what we have said is true, it remains so hidden for one reason — fear. Men fear being wrong, they fear the unknown, they fear change, they may fear straying from the truth. In general man prefers plodding along the well-worn path of familiarity to trail blazing new pathways of truth and understanding ."

Chapter Twenty-Nine

Rebekah sat with Elisabeth in church that next Sunday. Dr. Aziz was teaching at a church across the city. Rebekah no longer sat in church with her head bent down in shame. Instead she sat upright, shoulders back, head lifted up, willing to look at anyone eye to eye. It felt good.

After church, Rebekah walked slowly along the road that overlooked the Nile. Over the last several months her schedule had changed. No longer was there the intense inner drive to work. Peace replaced anxiety, self-value replaced insecurities, the sixteen-hour work days were passed on to others; her world was finally starting to make sense.

She arrived at the Aziz's the following week a few minutes late, rang the bell, and waited. Dr. Aziz welcomed her and they went into his study. "Now I have a question for you, Rebekah." Dr. Aziz began, "Where do we go from here?"

"I am not sure I understand. What do you mean?"

"Knowing truth is one thing, but living it is quite another. How do you intend to implement what you have learned?"

"The most important thing to me is not that I can now fight my way into some position of leadership, no. I feel validated as a woman. I know God has created me with certain talents and abilities and I want to use them to minister to others. I want to seek ministry not position.

"If the positions come along, then I will gladly step into them and do the best job I can. But primarily, I want to encourage and release others to be the men and women God has created them to be; working together, we can make a difference for the Kingdom of God." She looked directly at Dr. Aziz.

"You have learned the most important thing and I certainly did not teach you that. The Holy Spirit has been at work in your heart. Service and ministry indeed come first," Dr. Aziz noted.

"However, on a practical note," he continued, "let me share a remarkable incident that happened to me several years ago.

"I was invited to be one of the speakers at the Truth and Reconciliation Committee's annual conference in Capetown, South Africa. That was when Nelson Mandela was still president. I met him very briefly at a reception and was immensely impressed with the man.

"A few days later, I was invited by a friend to visit Robben Island where Mandela and many others were imprisoned. It is located seven miles out in the harbor of Capetown, it took about twenty-five minutes by boat to get there.

"If I remember correctly, he spent about eighteen of his twenty-nine years in prison there. The men who lead the tours and drive the buses that take you around the island are all ex-prisoners so their stories and experiences and commentaries were all first hand. We visited the actual cell where Mandela was caged — cell number five, I believe, the first one on the right at the head of the corridor. The cell was only about six feet square. A small window, high on the wall, faced the courtyard. The first years, the cell was completely bare, except for a thin straw mat to sleep on. Later he was allowed a small table.

"I was so moved by the experience that I purchased his autobiography and read it in just a few days. I asked myself, how could a man locked up in a tiny cell on a remote island eventually bring change to a vast and powerful government?

"The book was fascinating and many truths stood out. But one concept seemed to embed itself deep within my soul.

"When Mandela and the other black inmates first arrived on the island, they were issued short pants. All the other prisoners were given long pants. The blacks were not given any bread; the other prisoners received a daily ration of bread. There were many other acts of discrimination as well.

"While Mandela was caged in his small cell, he thought, 'I am out of the big battle; others will have to carry that forward. But I can speak up about the injustices I face every day. I will fight the small battles.' He fought for years to get the blacks to be given long trousers, equal food, and so on. I have never forgotten that. He fought the small battles that he faced on a daily basis and eventually won the war. That's something to think about, my dear."

Rebekah did not respond, but the look on her face told all. Her eyes slowly closed until there was just a small slit of an opening; her brow seemed to go in the other direction, until it was high and alert. Her lips moved together and out just a bit. She sat in silence. The point was well taken.

Just then, Elisabeth came into the room and Rebekah moved over to make room for her. Seemingly wanting to change the subject, she said, "I almost forgot. Next month, on the fifteenth, I have been invited to attend a reception, well actually ..." she shifted uncomfortably on the sofa and looked a bit embarrassed. "I am to receive a special presentation in recognition of my work at the hospital among the children with AIDS. It is really only a small gathering sponsored by one of the charities in town. I know you have a very busy schedule and I certainly understand if you can't make it, but I was wondering if you would attend it with me? It would mean a lot."

Dr. Aziz walked to his desk and looked at his calendar. Elisabeth noticed that he hesitated just a second, then asked again about the date.

"The fifteenth of next month," Rebekah responded.

Again Elisabeth noticed a slight pause. Then Dr. Aziz said, "Yes, of course, Rebekah, We can make it. It would be an honor."

After Rebekah left that evening, Elisabeth walked back to Dr. Aziz's office and stood at the door. Her husband looked up from his reading.

She walked over to him and gently put her hand on his shoulder. "Ishmael, are you sure you want to do this? I know how much you were looking forward to being the main speaker at the European Society's annual banquet next month. The ticket for Paris arrived the other day in the mail. It would be the grand achievement of your career to speak to so many of your colleagues; it really is a great honor. Rebekah would certainly understand."

Dr. Aziz turned slightly in his swivel chair and looked up at Elisabeth. "I am an old man, full of years and honors, probably more than I deserve. Now it is time for me to give back. Elisabeth do you remember how many of our children's music recitals, school functions, graduations, and holidays I did not attend? How many precious days of our children's lives I missed?

"I remember sitting in those lonely hotel rooms all over the world, holding the trophies of success, but feeling so empty inside. Those cold plaques and fading letters of recognition have brought me no warmth, no happiness, not like one hug or kiss from one of our children can.

"And now look at them. Those trophies collect dust in a forgotten corner. No, I have for too long chased these things that Jesus warned me about. Now I believe my heart and treasures are finally in the same place."

Elisabeth placed her right hand on Ishmael's cheek; she bent over and kissed him kindly on the forehead. Without saying a word, she turned and walked down the hallway toward the kitchen. A small, joyful tear trickled down her face; a faint smile crossed her lips.

Chapter Thirty

Rebekah had searched every part of the vast city; she was starting to lose hope. As she returned from a particularly disappointing day, she stopped by to see Pastor Habib. He was an oversized man in every way. He was tall, heavy set, with large hands and feet and a greatly enlarged heart, not physically but emotionally. He had long since humbled himself to Rebekah for not standing up for her. She had long since forgiven him.

Reverend Habib was still caught; he was only two years away from retirement. At the slightest provocation, Dr. Asbury would remove senior pastors and replace them with younger men, fresh out of seminary. If he was dismissed, he would lose all retirement benefits; in essence he would be destitute. Dr. Asbury knew this and used it to control the loving pastor.

"Pastor Habib, I don't want to get you into any trouble, but I am looking for a place where I can start the ministry I have talked with you about. Oh, I have a name for it, I am going to call it 'Arms of Mercy,'" Rebekah announced.

Reverend Habib threw his hands up and smiled broadly. "What a wonderful name, Rebekah. It certainly says it all." Rebekah could tell he was genuinely pleased.

"Please come in my office," he said. "I want to talk for a moment." Pastor Habib waved her into his tiny room. She chose the chair closest to the door; he sat behind a desk that was too small for him. He looked like a large schoolboy sitting at a child's desk. Rebekah smiled. His office was nearly bare. He had a few books on a shelf and a wilted plant sitting on a carton turned on end. Still, Reverend Habib seemed content in his humble surroundings.

"Rebekah, I have been thinking about your idea for reaching the street children. I cannot let it go, or maybe it won't let me go. I am not sure which it is," he said clearly pleased with his own humor.

"Anyway, I don't care what Dr. Asbury says or does to me. He is wrong, and I will not be bullied by him. Rebekah, I know a lot of people in our church want to help you minister to those children and I want to be a part of it as well. What do you need?" He looked at Rebekah with such compassion; tears welled in her eyes.

"The most important thing we need is someplace where we can bring the terminally ill children and at least give them some love and care and dignity before they die," she said honestly.

"Let me see what I can do," Reverend Habib said with a glint in his eye.

The following week, Rebekah received a call from Reverend Habib. "Rebekah, I think I have found a place. The church owns a property; actually it is the previous director's home, the one Dr. Asbury did not want. It was offered to my family and me. When I heard about it, I thought of you. There is a problem; Dr. Asbury must approve. To be honest, I don't think there is much of a chance of that happening, but you never know. Let's pray and see what happens."

Nearly a month went by before Rebekah heard from Reverend Habib again. He left a message at the clinic requesting her to come by his office immediately.

As she approached his office, he saw her coming and raced out to meet her. He did not say a word, but reached out with both of his huge loving arms and wrapped them tightly around her. He was crying. She had never seen her pastor act like this before.

"Come in my office, I have something to tell you." He almost pushed her in.

"You will not believe this. Dr. Asbury is leaving. The head of our denomination in the United States, Dr. Crockett died suddenly last week. The board of trustees has asked Dr. Asbury to return immediately to the States and take over as the interim director for the denomination. Word is, they want Dr. Asbury to be the next director. God forbid that should happen, but at least he is out of our hair," he said with sincere enthusiasm.

Rebekah sat in shock and disbelief. Could it be that her personal nightmare was coming to an end? She tried to imagine life without having to worry about Dr. Asbury.

No one was at the airport when Dr. and Mrs. Asbury departed. Thomas didn't pay much attention; he had been on his cell phone most of the morning with the headquarters in the States. He was already planning his first moves to secure his base of power. The denomination needed a major identity change; out with the old and in with something new. He had already been talking with a public relations firm to give them his ideas. Kathy sat quietly beside him on the plane; the pills she took earlier were working nicely. Her vacant, dull eyes looked ahead. She was drooling slightly, but Thomas didn't notice.

Rebekah used money left to her by Miss Lovejoy to furnish and equip the home that the church had made available. She closed her clinic and resigned from the hospital staff. The street children became her patients. Two of the elders, who had been at the meeting when Dr. Asbury had attacked Rebekah, came to her privately and promised to fund the entire ministry.

When children first arrived, Rebekah examined them carefully. Several looked terminal, but were in fact quite curable. But the majority were indeed dying. Helen quit her job as a social worker and joined Rebekah. She spent her nights on the streets, letting the children know about the "Arms of Mercy" house. Several women from the church brought food and clothing for the children.

The home for the dying was completely full. It held ten children. A full time staff of three assisted Rebekah and Helen: one cook, one housekeeper, and a nurse. Many volunteers came regularly, all women. Rebekah was waiting for the first man to volunteer. It was not easy, holding children while they died was very hard emotionally, so the volunteers came once every two weeks. Several volunteered to be on call for the children who would die in the night.

Rebekah had been gone for several days; a church in Europe wanted to hear firsthand about her work. She had just returned that morning. The gate bell rang. Normally the housekeeper would let the person in, but Rebekah was close to the door, so she went.

Two people were waiting on the sidewalk. Branches from the nearby bushes blocked her view; she could only see their legs and feet. As she opened the gate, Dr. Aziz and Elisabeth stood there.

"What a wonderful surprise!" Rebekah said as Elisabeth reached up to kiss her. Dr. Aziz stood quietly until Elisabeth and Rebekah greeted one another. He then bent forward and kissed Rebekah on the cheek.

"We were wondering if a broken down old professor and his wife might be of any service to you," Dr. Aziz said warmly.

"Come in! Let me fix YOU a cup of tea for once," she said proudly.

They sat and talked for several hours over lunch. The Azizes had visited Rebekah during the first days, during the move into the home, but they had not been back for several months. Rebekah proudly showed them the improvements made to the building and took them from room to room. Elisabeth kissed each dying child. As they came to the last room, Rebekah noticed a new name on the door. A piece of white tape had a single name printed on it in thick black ink.

Rebekah noted the new name as they entered.

"Hello, Simon. My name is Rebekah, this is Dr. Aziz and Elisabeth."

Suggested Reading List

For further in-depth study of this subject, the following books are recommended.

Why Not Women? by Loren Cunningham and David Hamilton, YWAM Publishing, Seattle, 2000.

How To Read The Bible For All Its Worth, by Dr. Gordon Fee and Dr. Douglas Stewart, Zondervan, Grand Rapids, 1982.

A Beginner's Guide to the New Testament, by William Barclay, Westminister John Knox Press, Louisville, 1995.

10 Lies the Church Tells Women, by J. Lee Grady, Creation House, Lake Mary, 2000

These books can be ordered from Rebekah Publishing's website. Go to www.rebekahbooks.com to purchase Rebekah, plus these excellent resource books. Or call toll free: 1-877-790-4588.

About the Author

Doug Sparks lives in Gunnison, Colorado with his wife Candy, daughters Stephanie and Elisabeth, and son Matthew.

Doug and his family spent nearly twenty years living abroad. Thirteen years were spent in the Middle East, the remainder in Europe.

Doug is presently a senior consultant for Development Associates International a leadership training organization based in Colorado Springs, Colorado.

Rebekah Publishing
Box 713 • Gunnison, Colorado 81230

To order your copy of <u>Rebekah</u> visit the website at:
www.Rebekahbooks.com or telephone toll free: 1-877-790-4588.

Ask about discounted prices for multiple copies for gifts, Bible study groups, Sunday school classes, or home discussion groups.

<u>Rebekah</u> can also be purchased on-line at:
      Amazon.com
      Barnesandnobel.com
      Borders.com

Ask for <u>Rebekah</u> at your local bookstore.